"Have you forgotten this is only pretense?"

"That doesn't mean it has to stay that way...."

"Oh, yes it does." Holly nodded fiercely, giving up all hope of avoiding this confrontation. "I'm not interested in any other way."

"You aren't interested in men, period," Zack told her grimly. "God knows seventeen is a vulnerable age, and I'm sure at the time you were hurt very much, but this is now. I want you so badly I've been unable to think of anything else all week."

"No...."

"It isn't the end of the world, Holly." He gave her a humorless smile. "If it bothers you that much, I'm sure I'll get over it," he added harshly.

He had no right to tell her he wanted her and then calmly tell her he would get over it! What sort of man was he?

Books by Carole Mortimer

HARLEQUIN PRESENTS

These books may be available at your local bookseller.

Don't miss any of our special offers. Write to us at the following address for information on our newest releases.

Harlequin Reader Service
P.O. Box 52040, Phoenix, AZ 85072-2040
Canadian address: P.O. Box 2800, Postal Station A,
5170 Yonge St., Willowdale, Ont. M2N 6J3

CAROLE MORTIMER

an unwilling desire

Harlequin Books

TORONTO • NEW YORK • LONDON
AMSTERDAM • PARIS • SYDNEY • HAMBURG
STOCKHOLM • ATHENS • TOKYO • MILAN

For
John and Matthew

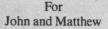

Harlequin Presents first edition March 1985
ISBN 0-373-10773-0

Original hardcover edition published in 1984
by Mills & Boon Limited

CHAPTER ONE

'. . . and I hope you continue to read and enjoy my books. You know the rest, Holly,' James dismissed with an abruptness that showed he was fast losing interest in the mail they were in the process of answering.

She looked up from her shorthand pad, frowning as she saw James was leaning back in his chair with his eyes closed. Her employer had seemed distracted all morning, hardly able to concentrate on the mail he usually took such time and care over.

'James?' she had to prompt softly, not sure if he wanted to finish now or continue; she had never seen him in quite this mood before.

He looked up at her, smiling slowly, as if her short red hair and small heart-shaped face dominated by huge violet eyes afforded him some comfort in whatever was tormenting him. 'Where was I?' he asked vaguely.

Her brows rose at this uncharacteristic loss of concentration, the same red as her hair, her lashes long and tipped with gold. 'You'd just finished thanking Mrs Smythe of Kent for her kind words of praise on your last book,' she reminded him gently, her concern intense for the man who had been kind to her from the first day she came to work for him three months ago.

'Oh yes,' he ran a hand through the dark blond of his hair, his hazel-coloured eyes half closed as if in pain. 'Could we stop now?' he sighed. 'I—I have a headache.'

'Of course.' She instantly closed her shorthand pad, moving with a quiet grace to pick up the two separate piles of letters from the table, one she had replies to and one she didn't. 'I have enough to be going on with,' she smiled reassuringly.

'I didn't realise I had so many fans.' He leant back weakly in his chair, his eyes completely closed now, a weary droop to his mouth.

Holly's heart went out to him and she wished there were something she could do to ease the strain he seemed to be under, some way she could help ease his stress. She liked this man, had taken an instant liking to him when he had interviewed her for the job as his secretary, and could only admire the way he got on with his life despite the disability of the wheelchair he spent the majority of his time in, the result of a serious car accident two years ago.

James was a big man, powerfully built and firmly muscled despite his disability, the pain of the last two years etched into his face and adding to his thirty-six years. He had the sort of fair hair that bleached white and gold in the sun, and it was like that now from the afternoons he spent working in the garden, his eyes taking on the blue-green of the sea that he viewed from his Hampshire home.

Yes, she liked this man, she liked him a lot, and she knew something was troubling him deeply. She hesitated at the door, not wanting to leave him like this. 'Is it just a headache, James?' she probed softly.

He sighed, opening his eyes again as he sat forward. 'No,' he admitted heavily. 'You might as well know, Maxine is coming back here this afternoon.'

Holly kept her expression bland with effort. Maxine Benedict, James's wife for the last five years, was a woman of thirty, having maintained her slender figure from her years spent as a model. In the last three months since Holly had been in residence as James's secretary the other woman had only spent a matter of weeks at home, this last trip to London being the longest so far, three weeks in duration. And now it seemed she was returning for another few disruptive days, would upset the even tenor of James's working days, and then leave him moody and withdrawn, unable to work, when she left again.

'That will be nice,' she said brightly, hoping James couldn't hear the lack of any real enthusiasm in her voice.

'Will it?' he returned bitterly.

'Of course it will,' she insisted briskly.

His mouth twisted. 'It's been so restful. I've been—comfortable, here with you the last few weeks, Holly. Almost at peace.'

She flushed her pleasure at his feeling the same way she had about his wife's latest absence, turning away shyly from the warmth in his eyes. She didn't welcome Maxine's return either. Beautiful and sophisticated Maxine Benedict made her feel ill at ease, and she suspected how the other woman spent her time during these frequent trips to London. She had a feeling James did too, although he never actually said anything about it.

'Oh, Holly, sometimes I wish—Never mind,' he dismissed harshly. 'Could you get those letters typed and back to me as soon as possible. I doubt I'll get much work done once Maxine is back,' he added ruefully.

Holly doubted it to. When Maxine was at home James's work schedule, and consequently Holly's own, went out of the window. Maxine was a woman of impulse, often deciding she wanted to do something or go out on the spur of the moment, and insisting that James accompany her.

Holly made her way to her own office at the back of

this rambling house, well away from James's study so that her typewriter wouldn't disturb him while he wrote. Once in the privacy of her own room she allowed her disappointment about Maxine's return to show, hating the idea of her routine being disturbed. She liked order in her life, disliked impulsive action of any kind. The next few days, at least, looked like being very disrupted.

James Benedict was a famous author of thrillers, the storyline often having something to do with racing cars, his old profession, the profession that had put him in the wheelchair. He had first begun to write during the long months he had spent in hospital recovering from the accident, and had been lucky—or talented enough— to have his first book accepted while still confined to his bed. A second, third, and fourth book had been equally well received, being fresh and exciting, and always original. The mail that flooded in to him every day proved just how popular with the public his books were.

Holly had been delighted when she secured the position as his secretary, thrilled when he asked her to assist him with his research too. It was all a welcome change and challenge from the run-of-the-mill office jobs she had been doing for the last four years, liking the fact that she actually lived at the house, finding it no hardship to give up the last in a long line of flats she had occupied during the last few years of living on her own. It also meant she was on call if James should need her, and the two of them often spent their evenings working too, something she enjoyed.

But the thought of Maxine Benedict's return was enough to spoil the day for her. Maxine was everything she despised in a woman, flirtatious, too beautiful for any man to resist, and worse of all, Holly suspected,

promiscuous. It was the latter she found so hard to
forgive in the other woman, but she could think of no
other reason for Maxine to spend so much time in
London. Personally she had no idea of the full extent of
James's injuries, although she thought it meant he
couldn't play an active role in his marriage, which made
Maxine's behaviour all the more abhorrent.

Holly deliberately made herself scarce in the house's
vast library after lunch, attending to some of the
research on South America that James needed for
further chapters. It was a laborious task, but one that
she enjoyed; no complaints were made by the public
about even the finest detail in James's books—
something she intended to continue.

She could hear the husky sound of Maxine's voice in
the lounge as she passed the room on her way back to
her office from the library, her precious notes and
references clutched in her hand to show to James later.

She came to an abrupt halt as she entered her office,
gasping as she saw the man standing across the room
from her, his back turned towards her as he looked out
of the window, the over-long golden hair so achingly
familiar. But he was *standing*! 'James . . .?' she cried her
disbelief. Surely James couldn't have been deceiving
them all this time——

The man turned slowly at the sound of her gasp,
dispelling any doubts she might have had that it was
James who stood there. Oh, the man's colouring was
the same, so was the powerful physique, but there the
similarity ended. Mocking green eyes steadily met her
gaze, a long hawk-like nose jutting out arrogantly, the
mouth strong and firm, quirking tauntingly as she
continued to stare at him, his jaw square and
determined. For all that his face showed lines of
experience he still looked younger than James.

There was about the man an air of male challenge, an aura of sensuality that made Holly's defences instantly spring into action. Her mouth twisted contemptuously at the way his denims clung to him like a second skin, his shirt partly unbuttoned to reveal the darker blond hair on his chest, an obvious move on his part to draw attention to his virility as far as Holly was concerned. A man who believed in his own machismo!

She stepped past him to sit behind her desk, realising as she did so how tall he was when she only reached as far as his shoulders, her own height only just over five feet. She viewed him with cool violet eyes as he lounged against the side of her desk, her lashes darkened with mascara, that and a coral lipstick being her only make-up.

'Obviously not,' she dryly answered her own question, completely in control again now, over the shock she had received at first seeing him.

'Obviously not,' he echoed mockingly, looking down at her, his gaze openly speculative. 'Not unless he's taken it into his head to get up and walk,' he drawled. 'And while he has people like you and his manservant fussing around him he isn't likely to do that, now is he?' he mocked.

A hot tide of indignation welled up inside her. 'How dare you say such a thing?' she gasped, her eyes wide with accusation.

His smile widened, his teeth very white and even against his tanned skin. 'Quite easily,' he taunted without regret.

'So I see,' she snapped, pushing her notes into a drawer and locking it before glaring up at the man. 'I don't know who you are—and to be perfectly truthful, I don't particularly care,' she added insultingly. 'But I find your mockery of a crippled man highly distasteful!'

'James isn't crippled,' his voice had hardened harshly. 'Unless you count his mind.'

Her eyes widened even more at this attack on a man who wasn't even here to defend himself. 'James has a wonderful mind,' she told him heatedly. 'As you would know if you've ever read any of his books!'

'I've read them,' the man confirmed scornfully.

'Then you know he has a clever mind!'

The green eyes narrowed; the man's speculation was increasing. 'Do you always defend James so— vehemently?' he queried softly.

Holly flushed her resentment. 'If I think he needs it, yes!'

'And does he often—need it?' the man taunted throatily, humour glinting in his eyes.

Holly glared her outrage at him for his implication. 'If you're a friend of his——'

'I'm not,' he stated flatly.

'Not . . .?' She looked at him uncertainly now, her eyes hardening with contempt as another reason for him being here occurred to her. 'Then you must be a friend of Maxine's,' she realised with sickening clarity.

Dark blond brows rose, his arms folded across the broadness of his chest, the red shirt he wore moulded to his powerful frame. 'Must I?' he taunted softly, mocking her unashamedly.

'Aren't you?' she challenged.

He seemed to consider for a moment. 'I suppose I must be,' he answered finally.

'I see.' Holly's contempt grew along with her anger. Not only did Maxine leave her husband to go to London for weeks at a time, but this time she had actually brought her current lover back with her. Couldn't she be content with hurting James at a distance!

'Do you?' The man watched the emotions flickering across her usually unreadable face. 'I doubt it,' he derided, shaking his head, the straightness of his golden hair growing well down over his collar and ears.

'Oh, but I do,' she contradicted with sarcasm. 'Maxine arrived from London a short time ago; you arrived with her.'

'And that tells you something, does it?' he queried softly.

'Yes!'

'But you're wrong. I didn't come here with Maxine, I arrived just after her.'

'Oh, she's given you your own car, has she?' Holly sneered heatedly, surprised at her own vehemence now. Of course it was disgusting that this man should be here, that he should have such little respect for a man like James, but she had made it a rule never to involve herself in other people's lives and problems, knowing it could only lead to disaster.

The man's eyes glittered a fierce emerald green. 'What a nasty mind you have, Holly Macey,' he said grimly.

She frowned. 'You know my name!'

'Of course,' he nodded abruptly. 'I was sent to see if you would like to come and join us in the lounge.'

She turned away, shaking slightly from this scene with a man whose identity she didn't even know. 'I still have some work to do before I finish for the day,' she refused stiffly.

'Don't you think you should come and defend James?' he taunted.

She blushed, suddenly looking younger than her twenty-two years. 'He doesn't need anyone to defend him,' she said awkwardly. 'He's perfectly capable of standing up for himself.'

'But he isn't, is he?' the man derided softly. 'Capable of standing, I mean.'

She gasped, shocked at the way this man continued to mock James's disability. 'That—that was a cruel and vicious thing to say!' she choked.

'Was it?' he shrugged, standing up. 'It's even crueller that he chooses to remain in that wheelchair day after day.' His expression was harsh.

'He *can't walk!*'

'You're right, he can't.'

'Then why *mock* him?' she breathed raggedly.

'Because I damn well refuse to pity him! He's a coward and a——'

'James is not a coward!' Her hands clenched and unclenched at her sides.

The man gave her a cold stare before walking to the door. 'The day he gets out of that chair and walks will be the day I no longer think of him as one. The reason he's there, driving a car at high speed just for the thrill of it, is a damned stupid way to earn a living in the first place,' he rasped.

'You consider your way to be better, do you?' Holly scorned.

His eyes narrowed. 'My way?'

'As Maxine's "friend".' Her mouth twisted with distaste.

'At least I get job satisfaction!'

'You're disgusting!' she paled.

To her chagrin he began to laugh softly. 'I'd be damned angry at the assumptions you've made about Maxine and me if I didn't find you so amusing. James only writes sexy thrillers, Holly, you don't have to believe them,' he taunted. 'And why do you have such a low opinion of Maxine?' he sobered. 'What has she ever done to you?'

'Nothing,' she answered stiffly.

Those deeply green eyes narrowed thoughtfully, his lashes ridiculously long for a man. 'But you don't like her, do you?' he probed curiously.

'I've only been here three months, I hardly know her,' she gave an evasive reply.

'Maybe you should remember that, Miss Macey,' he nodded grimly. 'You *don't* know Maxine. And you don't know me either.'

'I don't think I want to,' she spoke her thoughts aloud, seeing by his smile that he found her candour amusing.

'That's a pity,' he drawled with enjoyment. 'Because, like Maxine, I'm here to stay.'

'For how long?' Holly bit her lip, realising how rude she was being. After all, she was only an employee here, while he was an invited guest, for whatever reason. 'I meant do you intend to be here long?' she amended blushingly.

'I know exactly what you meant,' he drawled. 'And at the moment I have no idea. Why, does my being here bother you?'

She avoided his piercing gaze. 'It's really none of my business, is it?'

'None at all,' he replied smoothly. 'I'm looking forward to meeting you again at dinner, Holly Macey.' He left the room, whistling to himself as he went back to the lounge.

Holly realised she was shaking, giving up all pretence of working now she was alone. What a rude, insufferable man! His contempt for James had been nothing less than cruel, almost as if he thought it all James's own fault that he was confined to a wheelchair. And his affair with Maxine, right here at the house, was a disgrace.

She had never met anyone quite like him before. He didn't seem to take anything seriously, not even James's lack of mobility. He was a man who didn't seem to give a damn about anything. She disliked him as much as she disliked Maxine, and the thought of having to sit down to dinner with the pair of them made her want to eat in her room. But she knew she couldn't do that to James, he didn't deserve to have to face them alone then too.

She dressed with more than her usual care that evening, aware that it would no longer be just James and herself enjoying a companionable meal together. Maxine always dressed perfectly, with her figure it was hard not to, and Holly had a feeling Maxine's friend wouldn't be casually dressed either.

James's man Robert would make sure he was suitably well dressed. When she had first realised James had someone to help him out with the more mundane tasks like bathing and dressing she had wondered how he coped with the intrusion into his life, and yet Robert was one of those men who faded into the background when he wasn't needed, curiously always there when he was. The fact that Maxine resented his presence in the house at all didn't seem to bother either man, and as the married couple had separate bedrooms the meetings between the wife and manservant were kept to a minimum. Much as James loved Maxine, Holly wondered which would be the one to go, Maxine or Robert, if it ever came to a confrontation.

The dress Holly chose for dinner was the classic black, high-necked, long-sleeved, flowing loosely from the bust to just below her knees, her legs slender above the black sandals. Her make-up was still light, a pale lipstick, and yet her eyes remained her main feature, a darkening mascara showing the length and thickness of her lashes. Her hair was short and boyishly styled, newly washed, gleaming brightly auburn. Her lack of height prevented her having Maxine Benedict's air of sophistication, but all the same she knew she didn't look unattractive. Besides, who would notice her with Maxine about! It was enough that she felt confident about her appearance.

The lounge was empty when she walked in at seven-thirty, so she moved to the vast array of drinks on the sideboard to pour herself a small glass of sherry as James had invited her to do in the past if she should get down before him, turning back with the glass in her hand to find Maxine's friend standing in the doorway, a cynical twist to his lips. As she had thought, he had dressed for the part, in a white dinner jacket and white silk shirt, a black bow-tie and black fitted trousers, his blond hair brushed casually back from his face.

Holly stood her ground with effort as he came into the room, flushing almost guiltily as his gaze remained fixed on the drink in her hand.

'A secret drinker, hmm?' he taunted.

'Not at all——'

His soft laugh interrupted her. 'Are you always so quick to jump to the bait?' he mused. 'If you are, I'm going to enjoy my stay here this time.'

Her eyes widened at the implication behind these words. 'You've been here before?'

His mouth twisted. 'Many times.'

She should have realised that by the confident way he moved about the house. 'You haven't been here for the last three months,' she said stiffly.

'Not since you've been here, no,' he acknowleged derisively. 'Maybe if I'd known what a fiery secretary James had engaged I might have done.'

'I'm not fiery——' Holly banked down her anger. 'At least, not usually,' she mumbled.

'Do I take that as a compliment?' He moved closer to her to pour himself a large whisky.

'No!' Holly snapped.

'I thought not,' he said dryly. 'So you don't usually lose that delightful little temper of yours,' he murmured thoughtfully. 'What is it about me, do you think, that triggers off this rarely used temper?'

'You're insufferable!' she glared at him.

'Besides that,' he dismissed uninterestedly.

'Isn't that enough?'

He shrugged. 'I wouldn't have thought so. You disliked me on sight.'

'I'm sure many women find you very attractive,' Holly derided at his chagrined expression at the realisation. 'I just find you obnoxious.'

'Mm, novel, isn't it?' He appeared clinically interested by the fact.

She gave him an exasperated look. 'Don't you ever take anything seriously?'

'Life's too short for that. And I don't consider your dislike of me to be serious.'

'You conceited——'

'Not conceited, Holly,' he disagreed softly. 'I'm just intrigued by the fact that almost everything I say and do brings a heated reaction from you. James was singing your praises when I went back to the lounge this afternoon; I couldn't believe the cool competent young lady he was describing was the same one I'd just met. You may be competent, in fact that determined little chin tells me you are, but you certainly aren't cool. I was wondering what it was about me that brings about this Jekyll and Hyde change in character.'

'I told you, I find you insufferable.'

'And I told you it isn't enough.' He studied her through narrowed green eyes. 'Maybe it's my similarity to James you dislike. You defend him like a cat defending its kitten. I wonder——'

'Would you please pour me another sherry?' she requested stiffly.

He took the glass she held out, his eyes mocking as he refilled it. 'I thought you weren't a secret drinker?'

'I'm not!'

He looked pointedly at the second sherry which she had almost consumed. 'I hope that isn't on a completely empty stomach. Which way do you go when you're drunk, happy or sad?'

Holly paled at the taunt, slamming the glass down on the table, spilling some of its contents on the polished surface. 'I have never been drunk,' she told him tautly. 'Never!'

His eyes widened at her unwarranted vehemence. 'Holly——'

'Ah, Zack darling!' Maxine Benedict floated into the room, her black hair brushed in casual waves to her shoulders, her make-up perfect, the black dress she wore clinging suggestively to her model-thin figure. The contrast, in the style and wearer of the two black gowns, had the effect of making Holly's look nun-like! 'Pour me a drink, darling, you know what I like. Hello, Holly,' she greeted with her usual friendliness. 'What happened to you this afternoon?'

Holly gave the other woman a startled look, glancing briefly at the man she now knew was called Zack. His deliberately bland expression didn't help her at all! 'Happened?' she enquired abruptly, wondering what on earth reason the man Zack had given for her not joining them this afternoon.

Maxine accepted her drink with a warm smile before

once more looking at Holly. 'Zack came to look for you. James was quite worried when he came back and said he couldn't find you,' she added derisively.

'I—er——' Holly gave Zack an angry glare, receiving only a mocking smile in return. 'I was in the library.'

'What a pity I didn't think to look there,' drawled Zack. 'I'd been looking forward to meeting you.'

'Really?' she answered coldly.

'Stop teasing her, Zack,' Maxine cut in irritably. 'What on earth can be keeping James?' she added impatiently. 'Probably Robert can't decide which tie he's to wear.'

Holly's mouth tightened resentfully at the derision Maxine didn't even try to hide. She didn't know why the other woman came home at all if she was going to act like this. 'Maybe he would have welcomed your opinion,' she defended icily.

'He has only to ask,' Maxine told her in a bored voice.

That was the trouble, James would never ask his wife for anything, not her time, and certainly not her love. Couldn't Maxine see that? Or did she just not care? If only——

'Are your eyes really violet, Holly?' Zack asked irrelevantly.

She gave him a puzzled frown. 'So I've been told.'

'Really, Zack,' Maxine snapped tautly, 'the colour of Holly's eyes is of little interest.'

'Not to me,' he drawled. 'I've never met a girl who has violet eyes, I've only ever seen Elizabeth Taylor's in films.'

'Holly bears little resemblance to Elizabeth Taylor,' the other woman derided, her movements nervy as she kept glancing expectantly towards the door.

Zack gave Holly a long look of consideration. 'No, she's more like a red-haired Audrey Hepburn, all eyes.'

'Brings out the protective instinct in you, does she, darling?' Maxine's voice had hardened to scorn.

'A little,' he nodded. 'Maybe you should go up and see what's keeping James, Maxine,' he suggested softly. 'It's almost eight o'clock.'

Holly was becoming concerned with James's non-appearance herself, although she was more than a little surprised to see Maxine actually leave the room as Zack had told her to do.

'You can close your mouth now,' he drawled with amusement once they were alone.

Her mouth closed with a snap. This man gave the impression of making life a game, and yet he missed none of the emotions or movements of those about him.

'And maybe in future,' he added, dangerously soft, 'you should keep your opinions concerning Maxine and James to yourself.'

'I beg your pardon?' she gasped.

'You heard me.' The lazy humour had completely gone from his face and voice now, revealing a more steely side to his character. 'They have enough problems already, without a third person adding to them,' he warned.

'If anyone is an unwanted third person here it isn't me,' she snapped. 'You——' she broke off as she heard the descent of the lift from the bedrooms to the ground floor, a necessity with James's wheelchair, and turned away as the other couple entered the room a few seconds later.

James looked tired, more tired and strained than she had ever seen him. Her anger towards the other couple grew. How dared this man Zack tell her not to interfere when he and Maxine were the ones hurting James!

'Holly, my dear,' James greeted her with a smile. 'Maxine tells me you were in the library all the time this afternoon.'

She hated deceiving this man, and yet about this she had little choice. 'Er—yes, for a while.'

'But you and Zack have been introduced now?'

'Well . . .'

'There hasn't really been the time or opportunity,' Zack answered him.

James frowned. 'Maxine, didn't you——'

'Of course not,' his wife cut in sharply. 'The two of them were together when I came downstairs, I naturally assumed Zack had introduced himself. He isn't usually so backward in coming forward.'

'What must you think of our manners, Holly!' James said irritably. 'This is my brother Zack. Zack, my secretary, Holly Macey.'

His *brother!* That was the only part of the introduction that registered with Holly. This man Zack, the man she had been consistently rude to, was James's *brother.* No wonder she had confused the two of them at first glance, the family resemblance was such as to have easily made that mistake. But how could Zack Benedict have such contempt for his own brother, talk so scathingly about him getting up and walking?

'Mr Benedict,' she nodded abrupt acknowledgment of him.

'Zack,' he corrected smoothly. 'Or Zachary, if you prefer. But never Mr Benedict, Holly. Surely you're used to the informality here by now?'

Holly flushed her resentment as he very effectively reminded her that she was the outsider here, but she was restricted from answering him as she would have liked because of the other couple. Zack Benedict had deliberately encouraged her to believe her mistaken assumption of the reason he was here, was even now enjoying her discomfort, a taunting smile to his lips. But was she so wrong about his relationship with Maxine? Just because the two men were brothers that didn't preclude such a relationship between Maxine and Zack, in fact it could increase the possibility, the two men were enough alike to encourage Maxine to transfer her attention to the mobile brother.

She looked up to find Zack Benedict's eyes narrowed on her, as hard as emeralds as he seemed to guess her thoughts. Her head went back in challenge. 'Zack,' she repeated softly.

'Well, now that's settled,' Maxine put in waspishly, 'could we go in to dinner? It's hours since Zack and I ate in London.'

'But it was a delicious meal,' Zack smiled, grooves etched either side of his mouth. 'You have such a good cook.'

'Yes, I do, don't I?' Maxine purred at the compliment, smiling naturally for the first time that evening. 'You remember Abigail, James?'

'Of course I remember her,' he snapped his bad humour. 'I hired her!'

His wife flushed. 'It's been so long since you visited the flat in London that I——'

'I may be confined to a wheelchair, Maxine, but I am not senile!' he cut in harshly. 'Let's go in to dinner,' he decided roughly.

'James——'

'Dinner,' he repeated in an autocratic voice, a voice that brooked no argument from anyone.

Maxine was the one to walk beside the electrically operated wheelchair as they went through to the dining-room, and Holly had perforce to accept the arm Zack Benedict mockingly held out to her. Not that she gave him a second glance, being too taken aback by James's attitude to Maxine. She had never heard him speak to his wife like that before in her presence, and she could only wonder at his uncharacteristic sharpness with her now. Perhaps he too wondered about his wife's relationship with his young brother.

The small round table had been set with four places, one of the chairs being removed as James skilfully manoeuvred his chair into this vacant spot. Holly and Maxine were to sit either side of him, with Zack opposite, the younger man seeing both woman seated with a gallant flourish.

The meal was nothing like the quiet ones of enjoyment Holly and James had shared together in the evenings the last few weeks, James eating his food in morose silence, Maxine and Zack seeming lost in their own thoughts, Holly just feeling awkward and uncomfortable in the tense atmosphere.

'How is the writing going, James?' Zack finally cut through the soft clatter of cutlery.

'Fine,' his brother answered curtly.

'I'm sure working with Holly must be a great inspiration,' the younger man taunted.

'Holly is—restful to be with,' James replied slowly.

'Really?' Dark blond brows rose over sceptical green eyes. 'She doesn't make me feel that way.'

'Holly makes Zack feel protective,' Maxine put in derisively.

Hazel eyes sharpened suspiciously. 'Protective?'

'Actually,' Zack answered the other man, 'she doesn't make me feel that way either. Can you sing, Holly?'

'Sing?' she echoed in a startled voice, leaning back as her soup bowl was removed to be replaced with a clean plate for her main course. When she first came to work here she had been slightly unnerved by the abundance

of servants in the house, but now she took it in her
stride, although she was aware that the household staff
considered her to be apart from them, treating her more
like a guest than an employee like themselves.

'Mm,' Zack was watching her over the rim of the
wine glass he held cupped in his hands. 'With your
looks, some sexy clothes, and a good singing voice, you
could go far.'

'At least as far as your bed, darling,' Maxine drawled
mockingly.

'Maxine!' James slammed his glass down on the
table. 'Keep that sort of talk for your London friends,
neither Holly or I appreciate it.'

His wife's mouth tightened at the rebuke. 'But we all
know Zack's little songbirds occupy his bed at some
time or other.'

'You flatter me, sweet,' Zack said dryly. 'I have been
known to fail on the odd occasion.'

'I'm sure that neither Holly nor I are interested in
your prowess in bed,' his brother dismissed.

Mocking green eyes were turned on her. 'Aren't you?'

A delicate blush darkened her cheeks. 'I've always
believed that if a man has to constantly prove himself in
bed with a string of different women there's something
wrong with him,' she told him coldly.

'Such as?' He was still amused.

'Such as he really prefers men, he's very shallow, or
he's just afraid to fall in love with one woman,' she said
bluntly, looking only at him as she made the statement.

Maxine gave a laugh of pure enjoyment, her air of
bored sophistication leaving her for a moment. 'Well,
Zack?' she gave a gurgle of laughter, looking years
younger, a warm glow to her blue eyes.

'Hm,' he grimaced. 'You can safely discount the first,
Holly,' he said dryly. 'I enjoy and like women too much

for that to be true. The second? No, I don't think I'm shallow either. A little cynical, perhaps,' he admitted thoughtfully. 'As for being afraid of love . . .' he shook his head, 'I don't think that's true either. What's your excuse?'

She raised startled eyes at the unexpected suddenness of the question. 'Excuse for what?' she frowned.

'For not being married.'

'I——'

'Holly is only twenty-two,' James defended tautly. 'Much too young to be married.'

'I was engaged to you at that age,' Maxine reminded him sharply.

'That was different,' he snapped.

'Was it?' Her voice was hard.

'I think so,' he nodded grimly.

'How?'

'Maxine——'

'How was it different, James?' she persisted.

His eyes were hard as he looked at her. 'This is not the time to discuss it.'

'It never is.' She stood up with a noisy scrape of her chair. 'Excuse me,' her tone was brittle, 'I'm no longer hungry.'

'Maxine!' James' voice thundered across the room, halting her.

She turned slowly to face her husband, very pale beneath her make-up. 'Yes?'

'Sit down,' he ordered abruptly.

'Go to hell!' she snapped.

His mouth tightened ominously. 'I—said—sit—down!'

Maxine's head went back in challenge. 'Make me.'

James went deathly pale. 'Bitch!' he groaned in a pained voice, and threw his napkin down on the table, manoeuvring his chair over to the door, pushing it open with a crash. The room was starkly silent after his exit.

Maxine suddenly gave a choked cry before she too rushed from the room.

CHAPTER TWO

HOLLY had sat in horrified silence as Maxine challenged James's disability in that cruel way. Although Maxine was often absent from the house she had never heard the other couple be so hurtful to each other before. It wasn't——

'Stay where you are.'

She hadn't even been aware of standing up, just as she had forgotten the presence of Zack Benedict in the dining-room with her. She resented being told what to do by him or anyone else when they had no right to do so! 'I beg your pardon?' She looked down at him icily.

'Leave them alone,' he advised gently. 'From the look of them this argument has been a very long time coming.'

'But——'

'I said leave them, Holly.' He smiled to take the edge off his words. 'After all, there's no reason for us to miss our dinner too. James and Maxine's marital problems will have to be worked out between them. So sit down and we'll eat.'

'I——'

'I *could* make you,' he warned softly.

She knew he could too. Most of the time he was lazily relaxed, almost indolent, and yet beneath the superb cut of his dinner jacket and silk shirt she was aware of the powerful shoulders and arms, had more than once been a witness to the steelier side of his nature, a side he took pains to hide most of the time.

She sank slowly back into her chair, beginning to eat

29

her meal in silence. He might have 'persuaded' her to sit down with him, but she didn't have to give him the satisfaction of actually talking to him too.

She should have known the irrepressible Zack Benedict wouldn't be put off so easily. 'You never did say whether or not you can sing,' he prompted as they stood up to take their coffee through to the lounge.

'Not a note,' she answered absently, wondering if James was all right.

'Have you ever tried?'

'No, and I don't want to either! What are you, some sort of pimp for showgirls?' She made her tone as insulting as possible, still very resentful of his autocratic behaviour earlier.

He smiled his amusement, not at all put out by her insult. 'Actually, I'm a record producer. Disappointed?' he mocked close to her ear, sitting annoyingly close to her on the sofa.

'Not at all,' she told him abruptly, moving away from him so that the length of his thigh no longer touched hers. 'I'm sure you get just as much opportunity to show off your prowess there.'

He didn't rise to the taunt as she expected him to, but gave her a considering look. 'Why is it you don't like me, Holly?'

'Do I have to?' She deliberately didn't look at him, aware that he had shifted slightly, that he was too close to her once again, and her hands were beginning to shake because of it.

He shrugged his broad shoulders. 'You don't *have* to . . .'

'You just aren't accustomed to the novelty of a woman actually disliking you,' she scorned.

'Maybe later,' he drawled. 'But not usually on sight.'

She didn't need to ask what he meant by 'later'. His

hard good looks and lighthearted flirting might not appeal to her, but she could imagine a lot of women would be reluctant to give him up once they had known him. 'I must just be the exception,' she dismissed, standing up to put some distance between them.

'And maybe you aren't.' Zack stood up too. 'Let's see, shall we?' He moved purposefully towards her.

Her eyes widened in panic, and she stepped back to avoid him. 'No . . .!'

'Yes.' His smile was confident as he continued to advance. 'Relax, Holly, most woman enjoy it.'

His hands came out to prevent her moving any further, his head bending, and cool demanding lips took possession of hers. Her panic increased by the second, and she felt as if she were sinking, falling, her nails digging into his arms as she tried to cling on to reality.

'Hey,' he chided, raising his head slightly, 'I'm not into masochism!'

'Please . . .'

'Okay, Holly,' he shrugged, smiling wolfishly. 'Whatever you like.' He lowered his head once again.

She protested even as his mouth moved over hers once again, but even to her own ears it sounded weakly unconvincing. She thought she would faint as his mouth moved down to her throat, her breath coming in short gasps, only aware of his mouth and hands; his identity was no longer important to her, just that he should stop what he was doing. She reacted instinctively, bringing her knee up with all the force she could, hearing his groan of agony, as his hands fell away from her body.

It took several minutes for her to be under control enough to open her eyes, the only sounds in the room her own sobbing breaths and Zack's ragged ones. As she looked at him he was bent over double, obviously in a lot of pain, his face pale, a fine sheen of perspiration to his brow.

The full horror of what she had just done suddenly hit her. 'Are you—all right?' she choked, concern etched into her pale face.

He still couldn't straighten fully, and his eyes glittered with fury as he glared up at her. 'If I am it will be no thanks to you,' he rasped. 'What the hell were you trying to do?' he grimaced. 'Emasculate me for life?'

She watched helplessly as he collapsed down on to the sofa. 'Can I—get you anything? Do anything?' she queried.

He looked at her with jaundiced eyes. 'Haven't you done enough?'

She swallowed hard. 'I——'

'Brandy,' he changed his mind wth grim impatience. 'Get me some brandy—please,' he added dryly.

Holly hurried over to the drinks cabinet to pour him out a tumblerful, handing it to him with a shaking hand, taking care that they didn't touch again, seeing the derision on Zack's face as he noticed her evasion. 'Are you really all right?' she asked after his first gulp of the fiery liquid, noticing that he didn't even wince as it passed down his throat and hit his stomach.

He scowled up at her. 'I think I will be. God, woman, you could have damaged me for life doing something like that!'

She flinched. 'I—I'm sorry.'

'Sorry!' he repeated disgustedly. 'Believe me, if I thought I was going to be permanently injured I'd make you more than sorry. Who the hell taught you to do that to a man?' He took another swallow of his brandy. 'Your brother's idea of a joke or Daddy's sure-fire way of protecting his little girl's innocence?

This isn't the Victorian age, you know! And I was only kissing you, damn it.' He emptied the glass, scowling heavily.

'I don't have a brother, and my father is dead,' Holly told him quietly. 'He has been for years. I was taught self-defence during my last year at school.'

Zack's brows rose. 'Even the girls?'

'It was all girls,' she revealed dully, knowing what he would make of that.

'Now I begin to understand.' His mouth twisted derisively.

Holly blushed at the knowing look in his eyes. 'I'm not some repressed prude who despises men,' she flashed resentfully. 'You were kissing me against my will, I was perfectly within my rights to protect myself.'

'Oh, you did that all right,' he grimaced. 'I suppose you have a few other little tricks like that up your sleeve?'

'A few,' she nodded.

'Well, don't try them out on me. God,' he groaned his pain as he attempted to move, 'you certainly know how to put a man out of action!'

'Yes.'

He gave her an irritated look. 'You don't have to sound so proud of it. One little kiss,' he muttered to himself. 'Just one little kiss!'

'Against my will,' she reminded him tightly.

'You only had to say no——'

'I did!'

He sighed. 'Not very convincingly.'

'How convincing did I have to be?' Holly choked her disbelief at his arrogance.

'Okay, okay,' he dismissed impatiently. 'So you did say no. But how was I supposed to know it wasn't just a token resistance?'

'Do your women usually dig their nails into you?' she scorned.

A devilish glint entered his eyes. 'Sometimes.' His smile was mocking.

Her mouth tightened. 'On such short acquaintance?'

'Sometimes.' His brows rose in challenge.

Holly whirled away from him, knowing by his mocking humour that he was starting to feel better.

'Hey, where are you going?' he called crossly. 'I'm not sure I'll ever be able to walk again, and you just walk away! You might at least help me stand up!' He struggled to get to his feet.

Contrition for his obvious discomfort made her cross the room to his side, letting him lean against her while he gained his balance. 'I really am sorry,' she murmured as she saw he was still in a lot of pain.

'I'll bet,' he muttered.

'But I am!'

Zack gave her a sceptical look, straightening with a heavy sigh. 'Tell me something, Holly,' he gave her a sideways glance. 'Would James have got the same reaction if he'd been the one to try and kiss you?'

She blanched at the suggestion. 'Don't be ridiculous!'

Emerald eyes narrowed on her speculatively. 'What's so ridiculous about it? Or does the fact that he's in a wheelchair set him apart from other men?'

'The fact that he's married does that!'

'But unhappily, you have to agree,' he taunted.

'James is my employer——'

'And you think you're in love with him,' Zack stated bluntly.

'No——'

'Oh yes, Holly,' he derided mockingly. 'Maybe you see yourself as his confidante, his friend. Or maybe it's just his helplessness that appeals to you; whatever the reason, you imagine yourself in love with my brother.'

'That isn't true!' Her voice rose angrily. 'You're wrong,' she shook her head. 'Just because I didn't like you kissing me it doesn't mean I'm in love with another man.'

'Not just any man—James.'

'No——'

'Yes, Holly,' he insisted. 'Believe me, if I can see it then so can other people, maybe even James himself.'

'No . . .' Her denial was a choked plea this time.

'Yes,' Zack's voice was gentle. 'And you'll end up being hurt. James and Maxine may be a little mixed up at the moment, but they really love each other very much. You'll be the one left out in the cold in the end.'

'You're wrong about me.' She shook her head, backing away from him and making a desperate grab for the doorhandle, all the time shaking her head in sharp denial. 'You're only saying these things because of your own affair with Maxine. You——'

'My *what?*' he burst out grimly. 'Oh, I know you jumped to that conclusion this afternoon, and because your assumption amused me at the time I let you go on thinking it, but you can't seriously still believe it's true,' he dismissed scathingly.

She had the door open now, poised to take flight at a second's notice. 'Why not?' she challenged defensively.

'James is my brother!'

'And you obviously feel nothing but contempt for him,' she accused heatedly. 'You've mocked his profession, his inability to walk, why not add injury to insult and take his wife from him?'

He was breathing raggedly in an effort to hold on to his own temper, the steely side of his nature much in evidence now, his eyes glacial, his mouth a thin straight line above his clenched jaw. 'You can really ask me that in all seriousness?' he finally ground out.

Her chin went up defiantly. 'Yes.'

'Get out of here, Holly,' he told her in a rigidly controlled voice. 'While you still can,' he added, dangerously soft, as she made no effort to move.

Some of her confidence deserted her, and for a brief moment she wondered if she could have been wrong about him and Maxine. Then she remembered their closeness tonight, their intimacy with each other. No, she hadn't been wrong about them. But Zack was wrong about her, she didn't love James; she cared for him, yes, but she didn't love any man.

'I'm going,' she told him calmly. 'But don't think I've believed a word you've said. And if Maxine chooses you she's chosen the lesser man,' she added insultingly.

'Maxine made her choice years ago,' Zack bit out. 'She chose the right man for her.' He turned away, his earlier injury forgotten. 'Go to bed, Holly. I think you've pulled enough skeletons out of the cupboard for one night.'

With one last uncertain glance at the rigidity of his back and shoulders as he stared sightlessly out of the window she did as he suggested, closing the door softly behind her. Zack's last words seemed to indicate that there had indeed once been rivalry between the two brothers and that Maxine had chosen James. Or had she? Zack only said she had chosen the right man for her, that didn't necessarily mean James. Could it possibly be that Zack was so derogatory about his brother's disability because it kept the woman *he* loved tied to her husband?

She sat down shakily on her bed, remembering what else Zack had said. Could she really be in love with James? She hadn't thought she was. She cared what happened to him, was concerned for him, but was that love? She knew so little about the emotion between a man and a woman, although she knew her mother and father had loved each other very much. She herself had stayed away from emotional involvement with men since—since—God, she could still barely stand to think of his name, let alone the man himself!

Alex ... Alex Chance. He had hurt her more than any man had the right to hurt any human being, let alone one he professed to love. He was the reason she found it hard to love any man. She doubted if she would ever allow herself to feel those emotions again.

Neither James or Maxine came down to breakfast the next morning, although it was a Saturday, so perhaps that was understandable; James rarely worked on a Saturday, and Maxine was never an early riser. Zack Benedict didn't look as if he was normally the latter either, yawning tiredly as he came into the dining-room shortly after Holly.

She kept her lashes downcast, her gaze fixed on the cup of coffee she held in both hands, although she had noticed everything about him from the brief glance she had given him as he entered the room. He was dressed much the same as he had been when they met yesterday, tight faded denims and a casual shirt, the latter bottle green today, buttoned partly up his chest, the last three buttons left unfastened, as if he had been in too much of a hurry to bother with the rest. In fact he looked as if he had been in too much of a hurry to bother much with his appearance at all this morning, with his golden hair brushed casually back from his face.

'Damned razor,' he muttered as he seated himself opposite her.

'Hm——?' Holly understood as she looked up; she

had missed the piece of tissue sticking to an obvious cut
on his chin the first time she looked at him. Although
she shouldn't have done, it was large enough!

After the stilted way they had parted the night before
she had been a little wary of how they were going to
meet with any politeness today, but at the sight of the
bloodied piece of ragged tissue sticking to his chin she
had no hesitation in bursting out laughing. She had
never imagined she could ever find anything about this
man remotely funny, and yet the sight of him showing
such a human weakness as cutting himself shaving sent
her into uncontrollable laughter.

Green eyes darkened appreciatively as Zack watched
her with an emotion akin to amazement. 'Do you
have any idea what a difference it makes?' he asked
at last.

'Sorry?' She still smiled.

'When you laugh it's as if the sun had just come out,'
Zack told her softly. 'Beautiful.'

She flushed at the unexpected compliment. 'Do you
have any idea how funny you look?' she brought the
subject straight back to him.

He shrugged. 'Would you rather I'd subjected you to
the sight of just the horrific gash and my life's blood
slowly seeping away? Forget I asked that,' he grimaced.
'You'd probably stand by and cheer!'

Holly sobered completely now. 'Mr Benedict——'

'Let's not start that again,' he sighed.

'All right,' she nodded. 'Look, I know we got off to a
bad start, but if you really are going to stay here for
any length of time we can't continue to argue like this.'
She had thought this all out last night before she went
to sleep, and if she were to continue in the employment
of James's secretary she couldn't continue to be at
loggerheads with his brother—even if he did antagonise

her until she had to retaliate. Much as she disliked having to be the one to apologise, she knew she couldn't let things remain strained between herself and this arrogantly mocking man. 'I'm sorry I was rude to you last night. I—It was all a bit of a shock, James and Maxine's argument——'

'And then our own,' he drawled.

She flushed at the taunt. 'And then ours,' she acknowledged huskily.

'Why did you stop?'

'Stop what?' She gave him a puzzled frown.

'Laughing.' His gaze was intent on her face. 'It was as if all the lights went out.' He relaxed back in his chair, the delicate wood creaking under his heavy frame. 'You're right, Holly, we can't keep arguing all the time,' he said slowly. 'So what do you suggest we do, become friends?'

She swallowed hard at the husky implication behind his words. 'I was thinking more of acquaintances,' she amended.

Zack grinned. 'I've never been acquaintances with a woman, it might be quite interesting at that.' He sipped his coffee, giving her a sideways glance. 'Don't acquaintances ask after your health?'

This time the colour flooded her cheeks, and she almost choked over the toast she was eating. 'Are you— all right?' she asked as soon as she had her voice under control.

'I believe I'll have to take things easy for a few days,' he answered with innocent casualness. 'But after that I should be fine.'

His answer was so blandly given that it was all she could do not to laugh again. Zack Benedict really was the most extraordinary man . . .!

'Tell me, Holly?' he leant towards her with a serious

expression, 'do you think I've stopped bleeding to death now?'

Her lips twitched with amusement, but she gave the question serious consideration. 'Yes, I think so,' she nodded. 'Are you usually this forgiving?' She referred to his calm dismissal of the injury she had inflicted on him the evening before.

'Only with women who have Elizabeth Taylor eyes,' he flirted wickedly. 'Be a good girl and take this tissue off for me. If it looks like bleeding again stick it back on quick; this is my second clean shirt today, I got blood all over the first one.'

With any other man Holly would have shied away from this intimacy, but after last night she knew he would have second thoughts about attempting to kiss her again, possibly even third and fourth ones!

'What are you thinking?' He was watching her with narrowed eyes.

'Nothing very important,' she dismissed coolly.

'I'll bet.' He sat forward so that his chin was easily accessible. 'Those violet eyes hide a multitude of sins!'

Holly met his gaze steadily. 'Not as many as yours, I'm sure,' she replied tartly.

Zack gave a deep throaty laugh of pure enjoyment. 'I'm sure too,' he grinned. 'So how about taking off the tissue?'

His jaw felt firm beneath her touch, the skin rough from the beard that grew there. It was years since she had touched a man in any way, and she removed the tissue as quickly as possible.

'Tell me the bad news,' he grimaced, looking at her expectantly.

There was quite a deep groove in his chin, the skin looked red and sore. 'That's quite a nasty cut,' she told him softly.

'Mm,' he pulled a face, rubbing his jaw ruefully. 'For

some reason I didn't have my mind on what I was doing this morning.'

The way he was looking at her seemed to imply that she was partly, if not all, the reason for his lack of concentration. Holly flushed, attempting to move away from him. But not quite soon enough! The door suddenly opened behind them, the soft whirring sound of James's chair announcing his arrival before he spoke. Holly sprang away from Zack Benedict as if he burnt her, aware by the narrowing of James's eyes that he saw the movement as one of guilt, looking questioning at his brother, his mouth firm with disapproval.

'James,' Zack stood up lithely. 'How is Maxine this morning?'

Holly watched as James's face darkened, wondering why Zack Benedict felt it necessary to instantly antagonise his brother. The question about Maxine was inflammatory, and she felt sure the man seated opposite her at the table was well aware of it.

'I have no idea,' James snapped. 'As usual I doubt if we'll be honoured with her presence until lunchtime. I came to see if you would mind working this morning, Holly?' he looked at her.

'I——'

'On a Saturday, James?' the other man taunted. 'Give the poor girl a break!'

'Holly?' James demanded stiffly, ignoring his brother.

He was no less strained today, in fact if anything he looked worse. Obviously he and Maxine were still at odds with each other. Holly often worked with James on a Saturday, although with his wife back she hadn't expected to do so today.

'Why don't you have some breakfast first?' Zack suggested before she could make any reply. 'Relax a little,' he encouraged.

Hazel eyes were coldly angry as James looked at his brother. 'I relaxed yesterday, now it's time to get back to work. Holly?' He gave her a hard stare.

She pushed back her chair and stood up. 'I'm ready whenever you are.'

'Now,' he rasped, turning his chair to leave the room, clearly expecting her to follow him.

Holly watched his departure with hurt in her wide violet eyes. James had never spoken to her like this before, although she realised Zack Benedict's taunts hadn't helped to improve the other man's already volcanic mood.

'I shouldn't keep him waiting,' Zack murmured mockingly. 'He's likely to explode!'

She gave him a resentful look for his amusement. 'You didn't exactly help the situation!'

His brows rose. 'Was I supposed to?'

'James is your brother——'

'And yesterday and today are the first times I've seen him show any real damned emotion in the years since his accident!' he rasped. 'I'll do anything in my power to make that continue.'

'Even if you hurt him in the process?'

'Yes,' his eyes glittered, 'even if I hurt him. At least that way I know he's alive!'

'Zack . . .?' She looked at him with puzzled eyes, not understanding his vehemence.

'Go and do your work, Holly, and don't worry about my goading James; I know what I'm doing.'

She left him with a worried frown and went slowly down to James's study, moving quickly and quietly behind the desk she used when in there as he looked up with a scowl. 'Sorry,' she mumbled as he made no effort to speak.

'For what?' he bit out.

'I—Well, for—I'm not too sure,' she finished awkwardly. 'You seem angry about something.'

James gave a heavy sigh, relaxing a little. 'Just how friendly have you and Zack become since he arrived yesterday?'

'I—I beg your pardon?' She gave a deep frown.

He seemed to be avoiding looking at her directly. 'I happen to care a great deal for Zack——'

'He cares for you too.' She had no doubt about that now, was convinced he covered that caring with taunts and jibes that would bring about a reaction in James— any reaction. She didn't understand such caring herself, but James and Zack seemed to understand each other very well.

'Yes,' James acknowledged with impatience. 'And it isn't just because we're brothers; we genuinely care for each other. It's because I know Zack so well that I also know you shouldn't become involved with him.'

'But I——'

'Zack changes his women so often I think sometimes even he gets them confused,' James continued grimly. 'He's a flirtatious charmer, and if you become involved with him he'd only succeed in hurting you.'

'But I'm not in the least interested in him!' she at last managed to say exasperatedly.

He shook his head. 'I saw how close the two of you were just now, and I'm sure Zack didn't waste his time alone with you last night.'

'You know Maxine left straight after you did?' Her eyes were wide.

'Yes,' he nodded grimly. 'She came to my room in the hope of having a slanging match; I refused to assist her. Surely you've realised my marriage is falling apart, Holly?'

'I'm sure that if the two of you talked——'

'We would get nowhere,' he finished firmly. 'Maxine is no longer the type of wife I need, and we both know it. It's only a question of time before we separate for good.'

'I—I'm sorry,' she said in a pained voice, knowing how much this irrevocable breakdown must be hurting him. 'If there's anything I can do——'

'Stay with me, Holly.' His expression was intent, one of his hands coming out to grasp hers firmly. 'Stay with me,' he repeated softly. 'I need you.'

She didn't know how to answer him, wasn't able to, as she saw a slight movement out of the corner of her eye, suddenly seeing Zack Benedict as he strolled casually through the garden. The french doors from this room opened out into the garden, and they were open now. How much of the conversation had Zack Benedict heard? If he had heard any of it at all he must find it very amusing, each brother now having warned her about the other. Although it looked as if his warning about James wasn't altogether unwarranted. The question was, what was she going to do about it!

'I'll be your secretary for as long as you want me to,' she was deliberately naïve. 'You know I enjoy working here.'

'That wasn't quite what I meant,' James scowled his impatience. 'I want——'

'Sorry to interrupt you, James,' Zack spoke in a voice that said he wasn't sorry at all, as he walked in from the sunlit garden, 'but I just thought I should let you know that I'm driving Maxine into town for an hour; she needs to buy some things she forgot in London. I didn't interrupt you—working, did I?' He raised blond brows at Holly's hand still clasped in his brother's.

Holly removed her hand with a guilty blush, knowing

by the mockery in the dark green eyes that he had chosen to misunderstand the situation. He had no reason to condemn her on so little, not when he was so obviously more than a brother-in-law to the beautiful Maxine! She noticed the green eyes narrow slightly, almost as if he had been able to read her thoughts. Well, she didn't care if he had, she had been doing nothing wrong when he came into the room.

'Maxine is up, then?' James didn't bother to answer his brother's question, asking one of his own.

'Well, I could hardly be taking her into town if she weren't,' Zack baited.

James's scowl deepened. 'Why doesn't she drive herself? You aren't a taxi service.'

'It just so happens that I offered to drive her,' the other man told him sharply. 'It is her first day here,' he added abruptly. 'I thought she could do with the company. Unless you . . .?'

'No,' James rasped. 'Holly and I have some work to do.'

Mocking green eyes raked over her assessingly, almost as if Zack Benedict were accusing her of something. It wasn't too difficult to imagine what, not after what he had seen and heard! How could she possibly claim her innocence after this?

He nodded slightly. 'I'll leave you to it, then. Don't work too hard.' He left the same way he had entered, leaving an awkward silence behind him.

Holly didn't know whether to be grateful or angry at his interruption, knowing by his attitude that he had chosen to misunderstand what he had heard.

'Where were we?' asked James with impatience.

'We were going to do some work on the book,' she said briskly, wanting to divert his attention away from what they had really been discussing. She stood up. 'I

have the research notes you wanted in my desk, I'll go
and get them.'

'Holly——'

'Yes?' She turned at the door, willing him not to tell
her again how much he needed her.

He seemed to hesitate, then he nodded. 'Go and get
the notes,' he said gruffly.

She escaped the room with relief, leaning back
against the door for several seconds, then moving
quickly to her office as she realised James would
become concerned with the passing of time.

She had unlocked her desk and taken the papers out
of the drawer when her office door opened without
warning. Zack Benedict entered the room, closing the
door to lean back against it, his arms folded in front of
his chest.

Holly straightened at the blatant mockery in his face.
'What can I do for you, Mr Benedict?' she enquired
coolly.

'You can tell me what you intend to do now that it
appears my brother thinks he's in love with you too.'
His eyes were as hard as the emeralds they resembled.

CHAPTER THREE

'You *were* listening?'

He gave her an arrogant inclination of his head. 'Perhaps instead of looking so outraged you should think yourself lucky that I was the one who decided to take a walk in the garden.'

Holly paled a little. 'Maxine . . .?'

'She is his wife——'

'If you think I encouraged that scene you witnessed with James then you're mistaken,' Holly snapped. 'You have no right to accuse me of——'

'I haven't accused you of anything,' Zack reasoned smoothly. 'I just want to know what you're going to do about this situation.'

She flushed. 'I'm not sure there is a situation——'

'Don't be ridiculous, Holly,' the usually lazily mocking man lost his temper with her. 'Of course there's a situation!' He glanced impatiently at his wrist-watch. 'I just don't have the time to argue with you about it now, you have to get back to James and I have to drive Maxine into town. But we'll talk when I get back,' he warned, opening the door. 'I may not have accused you of anything yet, but I will if you can't think of a way to sort out this mess so that no one gets hurt.'

'Mr Benedict——'

'Give it some thought, Holly,' he advised softly, all laughter missing from a man she had thought found humour in everything. 'Because this certainly can't go on.'

The room was curiously silent and empty after he had

47

gone, and Holly knew that although she had done nothing personally to merit his anger he had a perfect right to feel it. The whole situation was turning into a farce, and she was going to be the innocent victim if she wasn't careful. Once again! She had been blamed for something that wasn't her fault once before, she couldn't let it happen again.

Fortunately James seemed to have forgotten all about the conversation she found so embarrassing by the time she returned with her notes, and with Maxine and Zack out of the house they were able to work steadily through the morning, James only calling a halt to it when he heard the other couple returning for lunch.

'I suppose we'll have to join them.' He didn't looked very pleased at the prospect.

'I'll just go and freshen up,' she nodded, no more eager to see Zack again than James seemed to be about his wife. And only yesterday morning she had thought how happy she was here; that idea was fast disintegrating.

Neither Maxine nor Zack was anywhere to be seen as she made her way up to her room, although she knew Zack was a man of his word, that they would talk some time today. Zack Benedict might not be anyone's idea of a confidante, but she knew she had to tell him her feelings towards James were merely those of affection, and if James had misunderstood those feelings she had no idea what to do about it other than leave here as soon as possible.

The atmosphere between the three occupants of the lounge was tense to say the least when she entered the room a short time later, still wearing the fitted black skirt and cream blouse she had worn all morning. Maxine's dress was as sophisticated as usual, its purple shade suiting her dark colouring. The two men were sipping what looked like whisky, surprising Holly; she could never remember James drinking in the middle of the day before.

His expression was darkly scowling as he put his empty glass down on the table. 'Shall we go in to lunch now?' he rasped.

'Oh, Holly and I aren't lunching here.' Zack was the one to answer, strolling across the room to her side, the mockery in his eyes taunting her open-mouthed surprise at his statement. 'We're going out for lunch,' he added as he turned to face the other couple.

To say they looked stunned was nothing to how Holly felt. This might be his idea of a joke, but she for one didn't find it funny. Although he didn't seem to be laughing either!

'You didn't mention this earlier.' Maxine looked at her brother-in-law accusingly.

'I didn't think you would be particularly interested in my plans with Holly,' he dismissed.

'Really?' Maxine was tight-lipped.

'Well, I'm very interested,' snapped James. 'Holly is my secretary, Zack, I don't expect you to come here and start flirting with my employees.'

'No one would have wanted to flirt with Miss Preston,' Zack mockingly named Holly's predecessor, a woman in her early fifties with a sergeant-major manner. 'You shouldn't have got such a beautiful replacement for her,' he drawled.

Holly hated the way he constantly thrust her in the middle of the tension between his brother and himself. 'I'm sure that if James would rather I didn't go out we could change our plans—Zack,' she added the latter awkwardly.

'No matter what he may have led you to believe to

the contrary, Holly,' Zack ignored the way she stiffened as his arm came about her shoulders, although one glance at her rigidly set features made him ease the pressure so that he barely touched her, 'my brother doesn't control your every waking moment. I believe even slaves had some time off.'

James became flushed with anger at the taunt. 'How dare you even suggest——'

'Calm down, big brother,' taunted Zack, guiding Holly towards the door, whether she wanted to go or not. 'You had Holly this morning, now it's my turn.'

She waited only as long as it took him to close the door behind them before turning on him angrily. 'I do not want to have lunch with you,' she burst out fiercely. 'And I do not like your innuendoes about your brother and myself. We spent the entire morning working, and I——'

'Calm down,' he gave her the same advice he had given James seconds earlier. 'I'm quite sure you did spend the morning working, I'm equally sure you don't want to have lunch with me.' He was suddenly serious. 'But we have to talk, remember?' he said grimly, the jagged cut on his chin giving him a fierce appearance. 'You do remember, Holly?' he prompted hardly, all lazy humour gone now.

She was finding it hard to cope with this man's lightning change of moods, had a feeling that the lazy charm and mockery hid a dangerous will of steel, that he rarely exerted that will unless he felt it very necessary. At the moment he found it so.

'Yes,' she mumbled. 'Although you don't have to take me to lunch. We can talk here.'

'I'd prefer it if we didn't.' He gave her a critical look. 'Do you have anything less—formal to wear?'

She blinked. 'Less *formal?*' She had never thought of the blouse and skirt as such.

'Jeans and a tee-shirt?'

Her frown deepened. 'Just where to you intend taking me for this lunch?'

His mouth quirked at her worried expression. 'Wait and see. Do you have denims and a tee-shirt?'

'Yes. But——'

'God, you're an argumentative woman!' he put in impatiently. 'Go and change and meet me here in five minutes.'

Holly would have liked to press him for more information about their destination, but the complaint of her being argumentative kept her dumb, going up to her bedroom to change. The denims were old and faded, very rarely worn, their cut and style drawing attention to the curve of her hips and the lean length of her legs; her tee-shirts were a little more numerous, as she occasionally wore them with a summer skirt, choosing a pale blue one with short sleeves, resting on her hips over her denims. Her reflection in the mirror showed she looked young and attractive, an impression she didn't normally cultivate. But nothing about Zack Benedict could be called normal; the man was a law unto himself!

'Much better.' He was waiting at the bottom of the stairs for her, taking hold of her elbow to guide her out to the car, a low green sports model that she had to climb down into, fitting his own long length into the confined space next to her out of familiarity, driving the car with ease out on to the main road.

The roof of the car was down and the wind whipped her hair about her face, although being short it didn't become tangled. She pushed her hair back from her face as she turned to look at him. 'Are you going to tell me where we're going now?' she asked dryly.

'Hm?' He inclined his head towards her, his own hair

completely blown out of style, gleaming golden in the bright sunshine.

'Where are we going?' she raised her voice.

'You'll have to speak up,' he shouted over the noise of the wind and the noise of other traffic. 'I can't hear a word you're saying.'

She wasn't sure he wanted to, damn him! 'Never mind,' she dismissed, irritably noticing he had no trouble at all hearing that, grinning as he moved away.

He was obviously enjoying the power in his car as it ate up the miles, the firm mouth curved into a perpetual smile of satisfaction, and lean strength of his hands and arms easily in control of the car's movements.

'Here we are.' He finally turned the car off down what seemed like a well-worn dirt-track, turning to grin at her. 'You're going to enjoy this.'

If Holly had expected a restaurant at the end of the track she was sadly disappointed. The track ended in a lush green clearing surrounded by huge oak trees. She turned to the man at her side with questioning eyes, only to find he was already climbing out of the car, a triumphant smile to his lips. 'Zack——'

'It's just as I remember it,' he turned to tell her excitedly, the green eyes alight with pleasure. 'We used to come here when James and I were children; it hasn't changed at all since then.'

There didn't seem to be much that could change! 'Zack, I——'

'Well, don't just sit there,' he chided with impatience. 'There's work to be done!'

Her eyes flashed a warning at him. 'Will you tell me what we're doing here, in the middle of nowhere!'

He raised dark blond brows at her vehemence. 'Having lunch, of course. Picnicking,' he announced as she seemed about to snap again, pulling a wicker basket out of the open boot of the car. 'See?' he held it up to her.

She shot him a look that threw daggers, and climbed out of the car with difficulty, smoothing her hair as best she could without benefit of a brush or mirror. 'You really know how to take a girl out to lunch in style,' she muttered as she helped him spread the blanket on the grass beneath the shade of a particularly lushly branched oak tree.

'Don't knock it until you've tried it,' grinned Zack at her discomfort, looking young and almost boyish. 'Mrs Ashley is a wonderful cook, and she prepared all the food.'

'That's something, I suppose,' she mumbled as she helped him unpack it. There was so much there, and so beautifully prepared, that she knew it couldn't possibly have been got ready in the five minutes Zack had given her to change. She eyed him suspiciously.

'And before you ask,' he sighed, 'I asked her to prepare it this morning before I went out.'

'Without consulting me?'

He shrugged. 'You have a way of proving difficult over everything, so I thought I would present you with a fait accompli. You have to admit this is better than trying to talk in a crowded restaurant.'

The reminder of the reason they were here had the effect of silencing her, and she continued to set out the food on the checked tablecloth with a thoughtful expression.

'Wine or fruit juice?' Zack prompted softly, the cooler open in front of him.

'Fruit juice, please,' she said instantly.

'I knew you would say that.' He placed two cans of juice on the cloth too.

Holly ignored his mockery, concentrating on enjoying

the food, feeling hungry after her morning of work. She secretly enjoyed the informality of the picnic, the peacefulness of their surroundings; even Zack's presence was not abrasive as he too concentrated on eating instead of goading her.

'Picnics aren't what they used to be,' he murmured regretfully as they repacked the hamper.

Her eyes widened at his almost wistful tone. The food had been perfect, the weather bright and sunny, what could possibly have been wrong with it? They hadn't even argued! 'No?' she enquired lightly.

He shook his head. 'The sandwiches used to be soggy, the fruit juice warm, and at least one person would get stung by a bee or ant. Those were the days!'

Her mouth quirked, until once again she found herself laughing at him. One thing this man did have was the ability to make her laugh. He really seriously looked as if he would have preferred the soggy sandwiches and warm fruit juice to the banquet he had just eaten. 'You've grown up, Zack,' she told him gently. 'I'm sure those picnics weren't really as good as you remember them, it just seemed that way when you were a child.'

'You're right,' he grimaced. 'I was usually the one who got stung by the bee!'

She burst out laughing again. 'You probably goaded that until it was angry too!'

'Probably,' he nodded, relaxing back on the blanket. 'How about you, did you get stung at picnics?'

The laughter left her face as she suddenly sobered. 'My parents both worked when I was young, so we didn't have a lot of time for picnics. After my father died when I was thirteen we had even less time for them,' she recalled woodenly.

'That's tough,' he murmured.

'You don't miss something you've never had,' she dismissed hardly.

'I wasn't talking about the picnics,' Zack said softly. 'It was hard losing your father at that age.'

'Yes,' she acknowledged tautly. 'Although my mother married again when I was fifteen.'

'Even tougher.'

She turned away, finding his understanding something she couldn't cope with. Losing her father and then having him replaced so quickly had been something she had found very hard to accept at the time, turning to Alex for the understanding she needed, until he too had let her down. Was it any wonder she had learnt to be wary of men and their intentions?

'Did you like your stepfather?' Zack probed at her silence.

She shrugged. 'He seemed all right. I didn't see much of him—I was sent away to school shortly after he and my mother were married.' Her voice was flat, showing none of the bitterness she had felt at the time.

'He was rich?'

'Yes,' she admitted dully, remembering the decision that at fifteen she should be sent away to boarding-school, the same school her stepfather's daughter attended, so that there should be no misunderstanding about her simply being pushed out of their lives. She had been pleased for her mother at the marriage, happy that at last the worry about money had been removed from her too slender shoulders, that her beauty wouldn't fade under drudgery. The adaption to a boarding-school hadn't been easy after years of living at home, but for her mother's sake she had done it. In the end it had been her salvation.

'Is your mother still married to him?'

'No,' she answered Zack woodenly. 'They were divorced several years ago.'

'Amicably?'

'Not exactly. I——' she broke off, glaring at Zack as she realised how he had been drawing her out. 'I don't see what business it is of yours,' she snapped. 'My family is my own affair.'

'Not if it influences the situation now,' he shook his head.

Holly frowned her lack of understanding. 'Influences it? I'm not sure I know what you mean?'

'I'm sure you don't,' he said dryly. 'But you've already denied loving James, and after the way you tried to evade the issue with him this morning I'm inclined to believe you.'

'Well, thank you!'

'Don't mention it,' Zack drawled. 'So if you aren't in love with him,' he sobered thoughtfully. 'I have to try and find out how you do feel about him. Knowing a little about your background could tell me that.'

'I don't see how,' she snapped her indignation.

'Well, you could see James as a father-figure——'

'At only thirty-six?' she scorned.

'Mm, it is unlikely, I'll admit that,' he said softly. 'Or he could be like an older brother. I take it you are an only child?'

She nodded. 'Except for the stepbrother and sister I acquired for a few years,' she confirmed stiffly. 'But couldn't I just feel compassion for James? Want to help him?'

'We all want to do that,' Zack sighed.

'Some of us have a funny way of showing it,' she taunted.

'Some of us don't intend to show it!' he rasped, his eyes hard.

Holly looked away, feeling rebuked in some way. 'Well, you don't need to worry about my feelings in this any more,' she told him curtly. 'I intend handing in my notice.'

'No——'

'I have to.' She stood up in jerky movements, walking over to lean against the tree they had eaten beneath. 'Until today I hadn't realised that James was—that he was——'

'Coming to rely on you emotionally,' Zack finished softly.

She shot him a resentful glare. 'Yes,' she bit out. 'This morning, if you hadn't interrupted, he would have—He almost told me——'

'Yes,' Zack acknowledged huskily. 'Whether he really means it or not, James imagines himself in love with you at the moment.'

'Whether he means it or not?' she frowned. 'What do you mean?'

'Do you know anything about James's accident, the extent of his injuries?'

'Only that it was a racing car accident. And that he can't walk any more,' Holly stated the obvious.

'Yes,' Zack stated harshly, his eyes narrowed against the glare of the sun. 'Shall we sit down again?' he suggested. 'We have a lot more to talk about, we may as well be comfortable while we do it.'

Talking was what they had come here to do, after all, delightful as the picnic had been. She followed him back to the blanket and sat cross-legged at his side.

'I've always wished I could do that.' Zack lay on the blanket beside her, leaning back on one elbow. 'I find it difficult enough at the best of times, after last night I think it would be impossible.'

She blushed deep red at the jibe. 'We were discussing

James,' she reminded him tightly, aware that although he might have forgiven her for last night he did not intend either of them to forget it.

His humour faded at the mention of his brother. 'James sustained a serious back injury at the time of the accident——'

'I already guessed that!'

'Let me tell this in my own way, hmm?' he mocked. 'I may not have such a gift with words as James has, but I do know how to do my own talking.'

'I thought you had only contempt for James's work,' she scorned.

'At the time he began it I think it was all that kept him sane,' Zack grated. 'And when he took such an interest in it we were all grateful; for weeks he'd just lain in bed, apathetic to everyone and everything. But I don't think any of us, his family or his friends, expected it to become his entire life.'

'You make him sound obsessive about his writing. And he isn't,' she shook her head.

'You didn't know him before the accident. You think I never take anything seriously?' he derided. 'James was the original daredevil and joker.'

It seemed difficult to envisage the grim man Holly knew today with such an image, so she wisely kept quiet. Zack knew his brother better than she did; she was beginning to realise that!

'Life was a game to him,' continued Zack in a preoccupied voice, his thoughts inwards, with the past. 'And he enjoyed every moment of it, met every challenge. All my life I wanted to be like him, and I always came a poor second.' He looked up at Holly with pained eyes. 'Do you have any idea what it's like to have your idol knocked off his pedestal in one blow?'

Her breath caught in her throat. Yes, she knew, she knew *exactly* how it felt!

'We all thought he would come out of it eventually, bounce back as he usually did.' Zack didn't wait for an answer, not seeming to need one. 'That he would meet this challenge too, start fighting back. He never has.'

'How can he fight his disability——'

'He doesn't have to be in that wheelchair!' he fiercely interrupted the gentle reasoning of her voice. 'The doctors told him long ago that there's no longer any medical reason why he shouldn't walk, that the injury to his back has completely healed.'

Holly was very pale. 'You mean he could walk again if he wanted to?'

'Oh, not instantly,' Zack dismissed. 'The muscles haven't been used for a long time, he would need physiotherapy, exercises. Unfortunately he also needs the will to walk, and he just doesn't have it,' he added grimly.

'I can't believe it,' she gasped. 'No one would stay in a wheelchair through choice.'

'James does.'

'But *why*?'

'Because he's safe there, no one expects anything of him,' Zack stated flatly. 'He's afraid to start living again, because he's afraid of failing. While he can hide in the wheelchair he can blame all his misfortune on that, the way he alienated all his friends one by one, the way he pushed his family out of his life, the way he's rejected Maxine. If he walks again, becomes completely mobile, then he has to begin living again. And he's afraid it's too late?'

'With Maxine? Or with his family and friends?'

'Both.'

'And is it?'

'I can only speak for the family,' he met her gaze challengingly, knowing what she had been implying. 'As far as I'm concerned he will always be my brother, and I'll always love him. I know my parents feel the same way.'

'And Maxine?'

He shrugged. 'She's had to take a lot from James the last couple of years, not least of all being his complete indifference to her happiness.'

'Oh, that isn't true,' Holly defended firmly. 'He always has time for Maxine.' James's wish to please his wife had interrupted their work schedule more than once. 'Maybe he's a little abrupt with her at the moment, but she was away for quite a long time, and he——'

'Did he notice?'

'Of course he——'

'Calm down, Holly,' Zack sighed. 'I thought we'd agreed not to argue any more?'

'Yes,' she acknowledged heavily.

'And you misunderstood me when I said James was indifferent to Maxine's happiness, there are many degrees of indifference.'

'But you said——'

'You misunderstood the way in which he's indifferent to her,' he raised dark blond brows. 'Just as there's no reason why James shouldn't walk there's also no reason why he can't fulfil a complete marriage. I trust you do understand me this time?' he mocked.

Only too well! She had assumed James was unable to be a husband to Maxine in a physical sense; she knew that the couple had separate bedrooms. Zack seemed to imply that this had been James's decision and not Maxine's.

'I can see that you do,' Zack taunted the hot colour in her cheeks. 'Any woman would find it difficult to live with her husband *choosing* not to sleep with her. From what I knew of them before the accident they were very close, in every way. Maxine naturally feels rejected, unwanted. In fact, superfluous.'

'A physical relationship isn't everything.'

'It can damn well help, though,' he grated. 'A lot of problems can be solved in the bedroom.'

It seemed to be where all of hers had begun, but she didn't tell Zack that. 'If you say so,' she muttered.

'I do,' he nodded grimly, surprisingly making no comment about her lack of knowledge on the subject. 'Unfortunately James and Maxine aren't sorting their problems out anywhere.'

'Well, I don't see how my staying on as his secretary is going to help. You've already said you think he's in love with me,' Holly frowned.

'Yes,' Zack confirmed. 'And James and I may be brothers, but with only two years' difference in our ages, we've always been great rivals too. For a while Maxine and I thought a little jealousy about the two of us might be what he needed to goad him on; James just withdrew more into himself. Now he's decided to settle for a nice safe love, for someone who won't demand too much from him, someone who didn't know him before the accident. If he thought he was losing that nice safe love to me he just *might* begin to fight at last. In fact, he's already started.'

Holly listened to him in incredulous silence, the full impact of his words sinking in. 'You aren't seriously suggesting—You can't want me——'

'I do,' he said firmly. 'He needs a incentive——'

'Well, I'm not it.' She uncrossed her legs to jump up. 'I'd rather leave than do what you're suggesting!'

'And ruin the little progress James has made the last two days?'

'I——'

'Do you really dislike me so much that you're willing to let him stay in that wheelchair?'

'This is blackmail!'

'Of the first degree,' he nodded calmly.

'But I don't want to become your girl-friend!' she said with obvious distaste.

'I can see that,' grinned Zack. 'And I wasn't suggesting it as a reality, only as a means to an end.'

'You say James is really still in love with Maxine, that he didn't react at all to thinking the two of you were lovers, so what guarantee do you have that he'll react to the two of *us* going out together?' she scorned.

'He already has,' he reminded her. 'And if he really thought he was losing nice loyal Holly to me he'll react even more, I'm sure of it.'

'It sounds cruel,' she said with reluctance for the idea.

'It's being cruel to be kind.'

'I doubt James will see it that way.'

'I don't care how cruel I have to be to get him out of that chair,' Zack told her grimly. 'I'll be downright vicious if I have to be. At the moment he's making himself and everyone about him unhappy. Maxine would have left him long ago if she hadn't thought it would do him more harm than good.'

'Ah!' Holly gave him a derogatory look, her mouth twisting with contempt. 'Now we're coming to the real reason you want James mobile; once he's out of his chair you'll feel free to take his wife away from him.'

'If I didn't genuinely think you believe what you're saying I think I'd beat you,' he rasped. 'But I happen to believe *you're* the reason they'll break up, if at all.'

'My involvement is purely unintentional,' she flashed.

'Will that really matter if the end result is the same?' he derided.

Much as she disliked his form of logic, it did make sense. She hadn't chosen to become involved in this situation; it seemed to have chosen her, James's behaviour this morning only confirming that she *was* involved. But she didn't want to be!

'I suppose not,' she agreed grudgingly.

'Of course it won't,' dismissed Zack impatiently. 'Now what do you think of my idea?'

'I don't like it.'

'Besides that,' he mocked.

She shook her head. 'It isn't something I can decide right now, I have to think about it.'

'For how long?'

'For as long as it takes,' she snapped.

'A week? A month? We don't have that long, Holly. Now is the crucial time, and we have to act on it.'

She turned to look at him, seeing his genuine concern. 'What will Maxine think of our—your suddenly becoming interested in me?' she asked in a weary voice.

'Just leave Maxine to me—Think what you like, Holly,' he sighed his impatience with her sceptical expression. 'You will anyway,' he derided. 'All I'm interested in at the moment is getting my brother back on his feet.'

Holly moistened her lips. 'I still need time. I don't——'

'Do you already have a boy-friend, is that it? If you do, you have my permission to tell him exactly what we're doing.'

'Thank you!'

'Is there a boy-friend?' he persisted.

'No,' she bit out.

'I didn't think so,' he said confidently, standing up to stretch his long legs. 'Maxine told me you rarely, if ever, take advantage of the weekends to leave the house.'

Holly bristled with indignation. 'I wasn't aware she monitored my movements,' she snapped.

His mouth twisted. 'She only mentioned it in passing. Oh, don't worry, you haven't been an unwanted third all this time,' he added tauntingly. 'Robert is already that.'

The hot colour wouldn't seem to fade from her cheeks. 'He had his job to do, as I do.'

'Maxine could do his job as well, if allowed to,' Zack dismissed that excuse.

'I doubt she could lift him——'

'Maybe not, but Mrs Ashley's husband could have helped out with that.'

'James doesn't like a lot of fuss being made about his disability,' she defended.

'Doesn't he?' his brother challenged. 'I reserve judgment on that.'

'How good of you!'

'Why it is that you rarely leave the house?' he persisted.

'I beg your pardon?' Once again she had been taken aback by his sudden reversal of the subject.

He picked up the blanket, shaking it free of grass before beginning to fold it. 'Your mother is still alive, isn't she?'

Her hands clenched involuntarily, making fists at her sides. 'Yes,' she confirmed abruptly.

'Where does she live?'

'London.'

Zacks's brows rose. 'That's only an hour's drive from here. Why is it you never visit your mother?'

Holly moistened her suddenly dry lips. 'Mr Benedict——'

'Oh-oh,' he gave a wry smile. 'We're back to that again, are we? I gather your mother is a subject you would rather not discuss?' he asked lightly.

'I——'

'Damn—what was that?' Zack suddenly dropped the blanket, looking down at his left hand. 'I don't believe it,' he muttered. 'I just don't believe it!'

'What is it?' Holly forgot that they had been discussing her mother, aware only that something was wrong.

He raised eyes that showed his incredulity. 'I've been stung,' he told her astoundedly. 'I've actually been stung!'

'Let me see——' She rushed over to where he was still holding his left wrist, a red mark already beginning to appear on the skin between the fine golden hair. 'What was it?' She gently probed the wound.

'A damned bee,' he growled. 'It must have got caught up in the blanket, and as I folded it the damn thing got loose and stung me!'

'Do you swell up? I mean, do you have an allergy to them?'

'Not so far, no. Although there's always a first time,' he added in a cross voice.

Holly's mouth began to twitch, although she did her best to control her amusement, knowing the sting must still be painful even though he didn't have an allergy to them. 'I'm afraid you would be angry too if you'd been trapped beneath a blanket and some two hundred and fifty pounds——'

'Two hundred,' Zack corrected indignantly.

'A heavy man,' she amended, '—came and sat on you. I know I'd be a little mad!'

He scowled at her, picking up the blanket to roll it up and throw it into an untidy bundle on the boot of the car with the picnic basket. 'Trust you to see this from the bee's point of view,' he muttered. 'I'm the one that's in pain!'

'But he's dead.'

'There is that,' Zack grimaced. 'Still, at least he didn't go in vain, he made you laugh, and my arm will be sore for weeks. Shall we go?' he suggested curtly. 'I've suddenly lost my liking for picnics.'

Holly sat in the car beside him, deeming it prudent to keep silent. After all, she hadn't been very sympathetic so far. Maybe if he hadn't been showing such an interest in her mother when it happened she would have been, but she didn't like it when anyone probed about her family. And this man seemed to enjoy delving into things that didn't concern him.

This time the silence during the drive didn't bother her, in fact she enjoyed the scenery. Zack had little time for anything but his driving, his grim expression showing that his arm was bothering him, although he wasn't going to admit it was.

Holly hid a smile, turning away. Men were such babies when it came to pain, she remembered the way Alex—All the sunshine went out of the day as she thought of him for the second day in succession, and after doing everything in her power to put him completely out of her mind. Working with James had seemed so without complications, now it was full of them.

'What are you thinking of?' asked Zack, as they neared the house.

Her mouth firmed. 'Your idea,' she said abruptly.

'And by the look of you no nearer to coming to a decision,' he rasped as he swung the car up the driveway to the house. 'Well, don't rush on my account,' he ground out as the car grated to a halt on the gravel. 'So far knowing you hasn't been too thrilling as far as I'm concerned,' he turned to look at her with blazing eyes. 'I've been physically attacked by you, almost cut my own throat while thinking about you, and now I've been stung by a damned bee. And all within the space of twenty-four hours! Being with you any more than I have to could be too dangerous to my health!' He got out of the car, slamming the door behind him before striding into the house.

Holly's good humour had somehow returned in the face of Zack's childish display of anger, and she smiled to herself as she slowly went into the house behind him.

CHAPTER FOUR

'So you're back!'

Holly turned sharply, blushing guiltily at the accusation in hazel-coloured eyes. 'Yes,' she answered James softly, all her amusement suddenly gone.

He deftly moved his chair further down the hallway towards her. 'I thought you and Zack were only going out to lunch; it's after four.'

'Did you need me for anything?' she frowned.

'Well—no,' he admitted abruptly. 'But that's hardly the point, is it? Didn't you take any notice at all of my warning about Zack this morning?' he scowled heavily.

'Well, of course I did,' she soothed. 'I was very grateful for your concern.'

'But you ignored it, anyway,' James snapped. 'Really, Holly, I thought you had more sense!'

'Than what?' she stiffened.

'Than to become yet another of the women who find my brother so fascinating.' He couldn't disguise his bitterness. 'If I didn't need you so badly I think I'd sack you!' He turned his chair and went into his study.

Holly was shaking by the time she reached her room. Zack was right about one thing, she had never seen James quite so angry and frustrated before. She couldn't pretend she wasn't surprised by some of what Zack had told her this afternoon; some of it had surprised her immensely. She had no idea that there was no medical reason why James shouldn't walk; she had thought his injury was permanent. Perhaps Maxine's attitude was a little easier to understand in the

68

circumstances, although her affair with Zack—if there was one—wasn't. If she agreed to Zack's plan, and by some miracle it actually worked, she could be leaving James open to even more unhappiness than he was suffering now. But at least he would be walking again!

Maybe she owed it to James to do this. She had been responsible for enough unhappiness in the past, she didn't want James on her conscience too. One marriage break-up to her credit was surely enough in anyone's lifetime!

After such disturbing thoughts she went and had a refreshing shower, then sat down in front of the mirror to perform the soothing task of drying her hair, allowing herself the time to think, to be aware of all the consequences being Zack Benedict's girl-friend would entail. The main drawback was that she didn't know if she was capable of being any man's girl-friend. There had been no one since Alex, and that had been years ago. In fact, it was the only drawback as far as she was concerned, because she really didn't want to be the cause of James parting from Maxine. But it was a big problem to her, and one that he would have to be aware of from the beginning. She hadn't heard him leave his bedroom yet, so she might as well go and tell him now.

Her light knock received no answer, and after knocking again she entered the room, only to come to an abrupt halt at the scene before her. Zack and Maxine were seated side by side on the bed, Zack wearing nothing more than a black towelling robe that left a large expanse of chest and legs bare, Maxine holding his hand as she looked up at him.

Both turned to look at Holly as she stood transfixed in the doorway. 'I—er—I came to check that your wrist was all right,' she spoke to Zack, unable to look at the other woman, knowing how ridiculous she must look just standing here gaping at the two of them. 'It doesn't matter.' She turned to leave.

'Don't go, Holly,' Maxine said abruptly, having stood up when Holly turned back to them. 'I only came to bring Zack some cream for his arm myself,' she held up the tube in her hand. 'Please don't leave on my account,' she added curtly. 'I have to go and change for dinner anyway.'

'Oh, please——'

'I'll see you later, Zack,' Maxine said brittlely. 'The cream should ease the pain in your arm.'

Holly stood slightly inside the room where she had moved aside to let the other woman leave, eyeing Zack uneasily, more than ever aware that he wore only a towelling robe.

He stood up, thrusting his hands into the pockets of his robe. 'Why did you really come here?' he asked suddenly.

She gave him a startled look. 'Your wrist——'

'Is the least of your concerns,' he drawled. 'You weren't exactly overwhelmed with concern earlier, so I can't believe it would worry you so much now that it would bring you hotfoot to my bedroom.'

'It wasn't "hotfoot",' she snapped. 'We got back almost two hours ago!'

'Exactly,' he said with satisfaction.

Too late she realised the trap she had fallen into. But when she had seen Maxine in his room, how close they were, she had changed her mind about agreeing to his plan. It suddenly hadn't seemed necessary for her to become involved, not when it was so obviously Zack and Maxine who were causing the rift between husband and wife, and not her at all.

'So why did you come here?' he prompted at her silence.

She thought quickly. 'I thought I should remind you that the picnic basket is still in the boot of your car; I didn't bring it in,' she told him, knowing how lame she must sound. But she hadn't been able to think of anything else on the spur of the moment. 'And the hot sun will make what food we did leave go off.'

Zack nodded. 'I'll see to it as soon as I'm dressed.'

'Oh, Right, I'll go and get ready for dinner——'

'Holly.'

'Yes?' She looked up at him with questioning brows.

'I'm still waiting for an explanation as to why you came to my bedroom.'

'I told you——'

'Holly!' His stern gaze compelled her to answer him honestly.

'I just—It's only—I thought about what you said earlier, about James, and I—What are you doing?' Her eyes were wide with alarm as he moved to close the door.

'What we discussed earlier was private.' He turned from closing the door, his eyes narrowing at her pale face. 'I'm not about to pounce on you now that we're alone,' he derided. 'I just don't want us to be overheard.'

Holly swallowed hard, nervous in spite of herself, unable to stop the inner turmoil this situation caused. Being alone with James in his office, or indeed anywhere, induced no such unease, and she knew it was because she felt no threat from him. Zack Benedict couldn't be dismissed so easily.

'Sit down, Holly,' he invited softly. 'We can talk now.'

'I don't think this is the right place——'

'You didn't seem to be of the same opinion when you decided to come here,' he reasoned. 'And where else could we be completely alone?' His mouth firmed at her sceptical expression. 'Maxine really did come to offer medical assistance,' he told her harshly. 'We would hardly go to bed together here!'

She flushed at his angry rebuke, although she still felt unnerved by the fact that Maxine had been here when she arrived. 'I came to tell you I want to help James, but after seeing you here with Maxine——'

'Leave Maxine out of it!'

'Can we?' she frowned.

'Yes,' he snapped.

Holly sighed, believing him. 'All right—well, I want to help James if I can.'

'But not be associated with me,' he taunted.

Holly glared at him for his perception. 'That's it exactly,' she bit out.

'The two go together, I'm afraid.' His mouth twisted.

'I'm beginning to realise that,' she nodded, telling him about James's reaction to them being out most of the afternoon. 'I've never seen him so angry,' she recalled with a frown. 'He really meant it about sacking me.'

Zack grinned. 'For becoming involved with his disreputable young brother.'

'It isn't funny,' she scowled. 'I could have lost a job I enjoy very much.'

'But you didn't, did you?' he reasoned. 'Which must tell you something.'

'Only that he isn't quite angry enough yet,' she sighed.

'Don't worry, if you should happen to lose your job I'll help you find another one.'

'Oh yes?' she mocked. 'I've already told you I can't sing.'

'And that you aren't going to comply with any of the

other requirements either,' he added tauntingly. 'I didn't have that sort of job in mind—we do employ secretaries too, you know. But at the moment I'm more concerned that James should continue to believe we're attracted to each other.'

'He's said nothing about your feelings,' Holly told him waspishly. 'Only warned me about becoming involved with you.'

'Then I'll just have to convince him that I'm equally besotted. Besotted,' Zack repeated slowly, as if he were surprised he had said it. 'It's an old-fashioned word,' he mused. 'But then you're an old-fashioned girl, aren't you, Holly Macey?'

'I'm not sure I'd say that,' she evaded.

'Well, I would,' he smiled.

It was the smile that did it. 'Why did you have to make it into an insult?' she flared angrily. 'Would you feel more comfortable with me if I'd had numerous lovers and cared for none of them?'

'I wouldn't believe it,' he shrugged.

'Which part?' she challenged, coming dangerously close to losing her control, and that musn't happen.

Zack seemed to sense how on-edge she was, and his eyes narrowed. 'Holly——'

'Which part?' she snapped. 'That I've had a lover? Or that I didn't care for him? Well, you can believe both parts, Zack,' she scorned. 'I've had a lover, and although I may have thought I cared for him I soon realised I didn't. There, do you feel better now?' Her eyes glittered with fury.

'Do you?'

She blinked at the softly spoken question. 'I don't understand——'

'Don't you?'

'No!'

'How long has the anger been building up inside you, Holly?' He was standing very close now, so close she could see the golden flecks in the green of his eyes. 'Since the affair broke up? How long, Holly?'

'Its none of your business,' she rasped, and turned away, stunned by his perception, learning more and more what a sensitive man he was. Most people would assume her to be bitter about the past, and although that was part of her feelings anger was predominant. Everything to do with Alex angered her.

Zack's hands came down on her shoulders as he turned her back to him. 'He must have hurt you very much,' he said gently. 'How old were you?' His eyes were narrowed.

'Seventeen,' she bit out. 'And yes, I was hurt at the time. But I've got over it now.'

'Have you?' he probed. 'Seventeen is very young to have been let down in that way. I can't even remember when I was that age!' he realised with surprise.

Holly's mouth twisted. 'I'm sure you were breaking hearts even then.'

'Maybe,' he acknowledged. 'But I don't think I hurt anyone as badly as you still hurt.'

'That isn't true,' she denied heatedly. 'I told you, I got over it long ago.'

'Holly . . .!'

She hadn't even suspected he was going to kiss her this time, wasn't ready for it at all. As a result she didn't fight him, but was aware only of the warm pressure of his lips on hers as he gently explored her mouth, his hands holding her lightly, as if he didn't want to frighten her as he had last time.

As she had always suspected could happen, she didn't want to fight him; she felt her body melting against his, knew the security of the lean hardness of his body as he moulded her to him. Her lips flowered beneath the insistent caress of his, her arms going up about his neck as she raised herself on tiptoe to deepen the kiss.

Zack's arms tightened about her, a deep groan sounding in his chest as she trembled in his arms, the hardness of his thighs telling her how deeply aroused he was.

She was aroused herself, her body aflame with need after years of physical denial. Her breasts throbbed under the slow thoroughness of his caress, suddenly taut beneath the clinging tee-shirt she still wore.

'God, Holly, I never dreamed——'

'That I could have feelings like the next woman?' The fiery pull of desire began to fade, her natural sense of survival once again taking over.

'No,' he shook his head, his eyes a dark green. 'No, not that. You——'

'This was a mistake.' She pushed completely out of his arms, sanity returning to leave her confused and upset. Admittedly no other man but Alex had come close to tapping the desire that was in her, but that she should have let Zack Benedict break through her defences left her vulnerable with fear.

Zack pushed his hair back from his face, its heavy straightness making it impossible to keep in order, especially when female fingers seemed intent on caressing it to disorder. 'I don't understand you, Holly,' he said slowly.

'I'm not asking that you should,' she snapped, knowing those few moments when she lacked control had completely changed her relationship with this man. And she was fast trying to re-establish the antagonism!

'But I want to,' he told her with obvious sincerity. 'You were a different woman just now, vibrant, sensual——'

'Do you usually have a post-mortem about a simple kiss?' Her eyes scorned him.

He flushed at the taunt. 'When it's with a woman who's shown me nothing but dislike so far, yes,' he grated. 'Maybe I should just think myself lucky you didn't try your self-defence on me again,' he added derisively.

'Maybe you should,' she challenged.

He shrugged, some of the tension leaving him, mockery returning to lazy green eyes. 'I believe we were discussing James . . .?'

'Yes,' she replied with some relief, knowing self-recrimination could come later, that for the moment she had to make this man believe her self-control hadn't slipped in that nerve shattering way. God, why couldn't she have shown him the same revulsion as the previous evening, why did she have to *respond*? 'I want you to realise that although I agree to your plan on principle, I do not want any more familiarity between us than there has to be.'

The mockery in his eyes deepened, clearly mocking her after what had just happened between them.

Hot colour darkened Holly's cheeks. 'I've already told you, the kiss was a mistake——'

'If it had just been the kiss I might have inclined to give you the benefit of the doubt,' he said seriously. 'But we both know it was so much more than that.'

'No——'

'I'm not going to push you into a corner, Holly,' he soothed, 'where your only choice is to stand and fight, or in this case, deny all knowledge. But I will kiss you again—soon. And you'll want me to.'

That was what Holly was most afraid of. She had discovered with Alex that she possessed a sensuality that shocked her; she daren't let any man take control of that sensuality a second time. 'I doubt if Maxine will approve of that,' she scorned. 'She may have agreed to your plan because she too wants her marriage resolved as soon as possible, but I doubt if she expects you to actually make love to me to achieve it.'

'Maxine has agreed to nothing—because I've told her nothing.' Zack watched her with narrowed eyes. 'She only knows what we want everyone else to believe, and that's that we're seeing each other.'

'But you and she——'

'Are friends, nothing more. I'll only tell you this one last time, Holly,' he said grimly. 'Maxine and I are *not* having an affair. We're friends, and I don't like to see my friends being hurt.'

'How about would-be girl-friends?'

He met her gaze steadily. 'Not them either.'

She turned away in confusion. 'So Maxine isn't to know this is all pretence?'

'No. She has her pride, Holly,' he continued. 'It's bad enough that James should think himself in love with you, without Maxine being aware that we're using that. How would you feel in her place, when she's loved James and stood by him all this time? Exactly,' he drawled at her look of contrition. 'Besides which, I'm sure James is only infatuated with you, because he believes you'll demand nothing from him, not even physical love.' He raised dark blond brows questioningly.

Holly's gaze dropped from his, her mouth tightening. 'You've already told me all this,' she rasped.

'Not all of it,' he taunted. 'Some of it I'm only just realising myself. Maybe you would have been good together after all,' he added hardly, his eyes like chips of ice. 'He wouldn't have asked what you don't like to give. You could have both stayed half alive then!' He sounded almost angry as he said the last.

But if he were angry so was Holly. 'I may have agreed to help, because of my affection for James, but I don't have to take your insults on top of everything else!' She left the room angrily, closing the door with a firm click. Damn the man, he got right to the source of a person's weakness and pain, and twisted his own particular brand of knife into it.

As she turned to go back to her own room she gave a dismayed gasp. A stony-faced James was looking at her with some disbelief. There couldn't be any doubt what he was thinking, not when she had just left his brother's bedroom!

'James, I——' she began.

'I believe it's almost time for dinner,' he told her woodenly, looking pointedly at the casual clothing she still wore.

'But James——'

'Excuse me, but I have to change. And it necessarily takes me longer than you,' he added bitterly, manoeuvring his chair to his room.

Holly let him go, realising in that moment how hard Zack must find it to be 'cruel to be kind'. It wasn't easy, but James's bitterness just now, completely uncharacteristic of him, showed that it just could work. If only she could stand Zack Benedict's perception for that long!

She changed without really thinking about it, her attention constantly wandering to the time she had spent in Zack's arms. He had enjoyed kissing her, she knew that, and the fact that she had enjoyed being kissed had been equally obvious. She had fought the knowledge of her own weakness for five years, a weakness that had cost other people their chance of happiness as well as her own, and if she had any sense she would run a mile from Zack Benedict. But she had already agreed to help, she couldn't back out now. She might have changed her mind about that if she had known what Zack had in store for her!

'Would you mind if Holly used the apartment in London next weekend?' he asked James after dinner. The four of them were sitting in the garden, the evening still clear and hot, only the sounds of the birds singing in the trees breaking the silence that surrounded them.

Holly's peace was at once shattered, and it took all her willpower not to choke over her coffee. She had no desire to go to London next weekend or any other!

'Next weekend?' James repeated slowly, obviously not thrilled by the suggestion either.

'Mm.' Zack seemed immune to the tension he had just introduced into an otherwise trouble-free meal, the conversation through dinner remaining outwardly polite, even Maxine and James refraining from snapping at each other; mainly because Maxine had been very silent this evening, seeming lost in her own thoughts. 'I promised Holly I would show her round the studio,' he gave her a warmly intimate smile, 'and next weekend seemed as good a time as any.' This last statement seemed to challenge anyone to disagree with him.

'The studio?' Maxine repeated sharply. 'But you've always refused to let any of us in there, claiming the work you do there is too important to be used as a side-show.'

Zack's hand covered Holly's as it rested on her thigh. 'I'm sure Holly isn't going to see it as such.'

She wasn't going to 'see' it at all. If they were going to continue with this it had to be together, not with

Zack making all the decisions! 'I wish you'd mentioned it to me earlier,' she began to make her excuses.

'I wanted to surprise you,' again he smiled.

He had certainly done that, and he knew it! 'It's rather short notice for me to plan to be away——'

'Your weekends are your own, aren't they?'

'Well——'

'James?' Zack prompted his brother.

'Holly is always free to make what arrangements she chooses for the weekends,' James confirmed stiffly.

'There you are,' Zack told her triumphantly. 'And you did show such an interest in the studio when we talked about it; I'd love you to see it.'

This man told lies and invented things without blinking an eyelid! She hadn't given his recording studio so much as a second thought since she found out that was what he did for a living. 'I couldn't possibly impose on James and Maxine's hospitality by staying at their London home,' she protested. 'It wouldn't be fair to them.'

'As far as I'm concerned you're quite welcome to use the flat in London any time you want to,' Maxine said waspishly. 'What I don't understand is the need for it. Why can't Holly stay at your apartment, Zack?'

His hand tightened over Holly's as she flinched at the suggestion. 'I don't think we know each other well enough for that,' he answered calmly.

'No?' the other woman challenged.

'No.' He remained calm.

'You surprise me,' she snapped. 'James tells me she wasn't averse to visiting you in your bedroom this evening.'

'She came to see about my bee-sting,' he challenged.

'For almost an hour?' Maxine arched disbelieving brows. 'That's rather a long time to enquire about one bee-sting,' she taunted.

Zack shrugged. 'I wasn't complaining.'

Maxine flushed. 'I'm sure you weren't!'

Holly couldn't help noticing the way neither Zack nor Maxine mentioned the fact that the other woman knew how long she had been in Zack's bedroom because Maxine herself had been in the room when she arrived. They must realise that James would definitely misconstrue that—and he would have every right to. Holly still wasn't sure of Zack's involvement with the other woman.

'Please feel free to use the apartment in London, Holly,' James told her curtly. 'If you'll all excuse me, I have some work to do in my study.'

'I'm going up to my room.' Maxine followed her husband. 'It's been a long day,' she muttered in a disgruntled voice.

'So James saw you leave my bedroom,' mused Zack once he and Holly were alone. 'What did he have to say?'

'Nothing,' she answered flatly, still angry with him for deciding she should go to London with him next weekend without even asking her.

'He must have said something,' Zack prompted with a sigh.

'That it was late and that he had to change for dinner.'

'That's *all*?'

'Yes,' she said abruptly. 'Now would you mind telling me why I could possibly want to go to London next weekend?'

'Because I'll be there,' he replied in a distracted voice. 'That was really *all* he said?' he frowned.

'Yes. Now——'

'But was he angry? Resigned? How did he sound when he said it?' Zack asked exasperatedly.

'Bitter. Zack——'

'Ah!' He sounded triumphant. 'Bitter, hmm?'

'Yes. Could you——'

'That's good,' he said thoughtfully. 'That's very good.'

'Zack, will you please listen to me?' Holly demanded angrily. 'I don't want to go to London next weekend!'

'Don't be silly, Holly,' he dismissed in a preoccupied voice. 'It's all been arranged now.'

'Without consulting me!'

'You could have spoken up at the time,' he dismissed with a shrug.

'While you and Maxine were having your private battle or afterwards?' she glared at him.

He gave her an irritated look. 'It wasn't private, both you and James witnessed the exchange.'

'Yes, and although you deny it, Maxine seems to feel she has some say in your actions.'

His mouth was tight, his hands thrust into the trouser pockets of his dinner suit. 'I've never made comment about Maxine's feelings, only my own,' he bit out.

Her eyes widened. 'You mean she *is* in love with you?' she gasped.

His expression was grim. 'Maxine is as confused as James at the moment, she doesn't really know what she wants.'

'But she thinks she wants you?'

Zack's eyes glittered with anger as he turned to look at her. 'She thinks she does,' he nodded grimly.

'And of course you've done nothing to encourage her into thinking that?' Holly scorned.

'No, I haven't,' he snapped. 'Maxine and I have been friends for longer than I care to remember, I can hardly deny her that friendship just because for the moment she's confusing it with deeper feelings.'

Holly didn't know what to say, totally confused as to what was going on now. Zack made it sound as if he was actually doing his best to discourage Maxine's feelings towards him.

'And before you jump to any more conclusions,' he rasped harshly, 'what I'm doing now I'm doing solely for James, not for my own benefit.'

'The thought hadn't crossed my mind,' she told him crossly.

'No?' he taunted.

'No,' she snapped resentfully, knowing it had been going to be the next thing that flashed through her mind. 'But why would you want to repulse such a beautiful woman?' she added curiously.

'Mainly because she's my brother's wife,' he bit out tautly. 'And also because I know I'm not what she really needs.'

'And James is?' she asked doubtfully.

'Before the accident Maxine and James lived mainly in London, when they weren't rushing off round the racing circuit. Maxine would find me pretty dull after that, I can assure you. Oh, I like to go out and have a good time too, but mainly I like to spend quiet evenings at home—some of them even alone,' he added mockingly. 'Maxine made her choice between us once, I think James was the right one for her.'

Holly didn't see how any woman could possibly find this man dull, but she had no intention of inflating his ego by telling him that. 'James feels she's no longer the sort of wife he needs,' she said.

'So I heard,' Zack nodded. 'But once he's out of that chair and walking again it will be different for them both, you'll see.'

'You sound so confident he will walk again.'

'Oh, he will,' he nodded. 'I just hope it's sooner rather than later.'

'You know I want to help him too, but going to London was not part of my plans.' There were too many memories there, too many people she never wanted to see again.

Zack sighed. 'It wasn't part of mine either to start with, but you don't act very much like my girl-friend here, so I had hoped James would think you were more amenable in London.'

'I've already warned you I won't be part of your familiarity,' snapped Holly.

'There's a difference between that and being damned frosty!'

'If you aren't satisfied then you know what you can do!' she glared at him.

'God, you live up to your name, don't you?' he said exasperatedly. 'Prickly as hell! I'm going back to London tomorrow night,' he sighed. 'Just try and bear with me until then.'

'I thought you intended staying for some time?'

'My plans have changed.' The hardness of his eyes seemed to imply that she was the reason for that. 'Just be at the London flat when I call for you at eight o'clock on Friday evening,' he warned.

'Surely we don't have to continue with this there?' she sighed. 'It's enough that James and Maxine believe we're seeing each other.'

'Eight o'clock,' he strode forcefully to the door. 'Be there.'

'But Zack——'

'Be there, Holly,' he told her in a softly controlled voice. 'Otherwise I could get nasty.'

'You don't frighten me——'

'No?' he taunted. 'Let's wait and see, shall we? If you

aren't waiting for me I'll come looking for you, and I may not be in a pleasant frame of mind.'

'Are you ever?' she said bitterly.

'Frequently. One of these days I just may surprise you,' he mocked.

'I doubt it,' Holly snapped. 'You're highly predictable!'

He shook his head, his mouth quirking with humour. 'Do you always have to have the last word?'

She gave a rueful smile. 'With you it pays to.'

Zack returned the smile. 'Maybe. I have been accused of being domineering from time to time.'

'Really?' she mocked disbelievingly.

'Yes—really,' he chuckled softly.

'I can't think why,' said Holly with feigned innocence.

'Neither can I,' he grinned. 'Get a good night's sleep, Holly. All this will seem more acceptable in the morning.'

But it wouldn't, she knew it wouldn't. Alex was in London, her mother too, and she didn't want to see either of them again. Alex had betrayed her, and although her mother had been hurt too she had let Holly down at a time when she needed her the most. She *couldn't* see either of them again!

Zach kept to his word and left the next day, much to Holly's relief, although her relationship with James stayed very curt on his side, and Zack's nightly telephone calls did not help. When he called for the first time on Monday evening and asked to talk to her she had expected a change in their plans for the weekend, and was surprised when he said he had just telephoned for a chat.

The calls continued through the week, and while she became a little more relaxed about them, Maxine and

James obviously reacted in the opposite way, Maxine being almost as abrupt with her now as James was. In fact, the weekend away became something to look forward to rather than dreaded!

'Zack is being rather attentive,' remarked Maxine after Thursday evening's call.

'Yes,' she replied without elaboration, not wishing to antagonise the other woman any more than she had to.

Maxine glanced at her husband. 'Perhaps we should have warned you about not taking Zack too seriously.' Her voice was friendly, but her eyes remained hard. 'Shouldn't we, James?' she prompted him.

He glanced up from the glass of whisky he had been broodingly staring into. 'Holly prefers not to take notice of warnings,' he rasped.

'Do you?' Maxine looked at her with hard blue eyes.

'I——'

'Because where Zack is concerned that would be very silly.' The friendliness of Maxine's voice couldn't altogether conceal the edge of steel it contained.

'I'm sure——'

'James and I know him so much better than you do.' She smoothed her black silky dress over her long legs, her hands slender and graceful, tipped with scarlet nail polish.

'I'm sure you do,' she said stiffly, relieved to at last be able to finish a sentence.

'His interest never lasts for long,' Maxine continued hardly. 'And it could make things awkward for you here when you're no longer—seeing each other.'

'Awkward?' Holly repeated abruptly.

'Embarrassing, then,' Maxine amended in a bored voice. 'Zack has always been a regular visitor, hasn't he, James?' Once again she prompted her husband to join in the conversation.

He turned from replenishing his glass. 'He always used to be, yes,' he scowled.

'He still is,' Maxine snapped irritably. 'He visits me regularly when I'm in London. He would visit you there too if you—Now there's an idea, James!' she brightened excitedly. 'We could go up to London with Holly tomorrow.'

James slowly lowered his glass, staring at his wife as if she had gone insane. 'What?'

'We could go with Holly to London——'

'I heard that,' he rasped.

'Then why——'

'I heard it,' he bit out tautly. 'I just couldn't believe you meant it.'

'But it would be perfect, James.' Maxine moved to take his hand. 'You've always given the fact that you would be too far away from your work as the main reason for not going up to London—well, now you would have Holly with you. I don't know why we've never thought of this before.'

Holly knew; it was because Maxine had never been this desperate to go to London before, to keep a watchful eye on her and Zack. The other woman was so intent on observing Zack that she didn't seem to realise that James's moroseness of the last week had been because of his feelings of jealousy because of another woman.

'Holly is not my work,' he rasped harshly.

'No, but you have to admit she could help you with it if you suddenly wanted to work while you're there——'

'Holly isn't going to London to work,' he snapped.

'But I'm sure she wouldn't mind, when she isn't seeing Zack. Would you, Holly?' Maxine prompted eagerly.

Holly's incredulity had been increasing as the

conversation progressed, mainly because James hadn't yet turned the idea down flat. 'No, I wouldn't mind at all,' she told them dazedly.

'There you are, James,' Maxine looked pleased with herself. 'It would be ideal.'

His mouth firmed. 'I need to think about it,' he muttered.

'What did you say?' his wife pounced, her face glowing.

'I said I'd think about it,' he repeated fiercely. 'And I will. I'll let you know what I've decided tomorrow.'

'Not too late,' Maxine encouraged as the two of them left the room together, Holly seemingly forgotten now that she had agreed to the idea. 'Because we'll need to make all the arrangements.'

'I won't be rushed,' James could be heard complaining in a disgruntled voice as they got into the lift together.

Holly sat alone in the lounge, her feelings mixed, pleased that James was at least thinking of leaving the house for a while, although she realised his reasons for doing so were not yet apparent to Maxine. How would the other woman react if she did know—be relieved that she could be free to pursue Zack, or finally realise that she still loved her husband? It was a tangle that only time would unravel.

CHAPTER FIVE

'How did you manage it?'

Holly turned to look at the man at her side. Zack was looking rakishly handsome in the white dinner jacket, white ruffled shirt and black trousers. 'Manage what?' she asked distractedly, London holding her attention as they drove through the busy streets, not looking as if it had changed much during the last five years, still the untidily sprawling city that she had once loved.

'To get James here, of course.' He seemed impatient with her lack of comprehension.

The four of them, Maxine and James, Robert and Holly, had driven up to London this afternoon, James having decided this morning that he would make the trip. Holly had telephoned Zack at the number he had given her earlier in the week but had been unable to reach him. Consequently he had been completely surprised to see his brother at the flat this evening when he arrived to take her out.

'I didn't,' she shrugged off any of the credit being hers. 'It was Maxine's idea.'

Zack looked somewhat less elated. 'Oh.'

'Mm,' she grimaced. 'I think she was a little concerned about what you were doing while she's away.'

'I was telephoning you mostly,' he scowled at her taunt.

'She wasn't too pleased about that either,' Holly told him softly.

His hands tightened momentarily on the steering-wheel, then he visibly forced himself to relax. 'What's important is that James came here.'

'Yes,' she had to agree with that, she had known he would be pleased. 'Although he claims he intends working—alone—while he's here.'

'It doesn't matter what he does,' Zack dismissed, 'as long as he's here. Next time——'

'You're very optimistic, considering it's taken over a year to get him here this time.' Her eyes were wide at his arrogance.

He shook his head. 'Just hopeful. Next time we'll get to work on him, try to get him out, things like that.'

Remembering the way James had disappeared into his bedroom when they arrived, and stayed there, she thought it might take a little longer than 'next time' to achieve what Zack wanted to achieve. James had looked very strained by the time they reached London late this afternoon, and she knew it wasn't just the journey that had tired him, that he had wanted to see London again with its hurtful memories as little as she did.

'You can try,' she agreed with little enthusiasm.

'That's what I like about you, Holly,' he gave her an angry glance 'Your optimism!'

She flushed at the rebuke. 'I don't get let down as much my way,' she said stiffly.

'You don't feel half as much either!'

She flinched. 'When I want your advice——'

'You'll ask for it,' he finished dryly. 'I bet you've never asked for anything in your life,' he scorned.

Holly recoiled as if he had hit her. 'You might be surprised,' she muttered.

'I doubt that,' he drawled, his concentration on the road ahead of them making him miss her pained reaction seconds earlier. Thank goodness!

'Where are we going?' Holly woodenly changed the subject.

'To dinner at one of my favourite restaurants.'

She couldn't argue with that, in fact she felt quite hungry; it was a long time since lunch. Zack was obviously well known at the restaurant they entered a short time later, being shown to one of the best tables in the room despite the fact that it was already very busy. Zack's 'favourite' restaurant came as something of a surprise to Holly, small and intimate, the tables far enough apart to allow their occupants freedom of speech.

'Very nice,' she warmly complimented him once they had chosen their meal, having expected something completely different.

'Surprised?' He raised mocking brows, wickedly attractive in the warm glow of the subdued lighting.

'Very.'

Zack laughed softly. 'I find your honesty very refreshing,' he explained.

'Oh, it is,' her mouth twisted. 'Unfortunately it just isn't "in" this year.'

'That depends on who you're with,' he held her gaze with his. 'I happen to prefer honesty myself. For instance, I missed you this last week.' He sipped the wine that had been poured for them.

Holly couldn't stop the blush that stole into her cheeks. 'No more cuts shaving, or bee-stings?' she taunted to hide her embarrassment at such a frank admission.

'None. Holly——'

'How is your wrist now?' she firmly cut across whatever he had been going to say.

'Better,' he dismissed, placing his hand over hers as it lay on the table, his wrist visible to her. 'See?'

She quickly removed her hand. 'Yes, I see. Very well, as it happens. Have you forgotten this is only pretence?' She searched in her evening bag for a tissue she didn't need.

'That doesn't mean it has to stay that way——'

'Oh yes, it does,' she nodded fiercely, giving up all hope of avoiding this confrontation.

'Why?' His eyes were darkly green.

Holly moistened her lips. 'Because I'm not interested in it being any other way.'

'You aren't interested in men, period,' Zack told her grimly. 'God knows seventeen is a vulnerable age, and I'm sure that at the time you were hurt very much, but that was five years ago, and this is now. I want you, Holly. I want you so badly I've been unable to think of anything else all week.'

Her breath caught in her throat and she had trouble breathing. 'No . . .' she finally managed to choke, shaking her head.

'It isn't the end of the world, Holly,' he gave her a humourless smile. 'And if it bothers you that much I'm sure I'll get over it,' he added hardly.

The arrival of their food prevented her making any cutting comment to his bland dismissal of a statement that had so upset her. He had no right to tell her he wanted her and then calmly tell her he would get over it! What sort of man was he?

'Sulking?'

'I——' she broke off as she looked straight into the depths of his mocking green eyes. 'Not really,' she sighed. 'But you're very disconcerting. You say you want me, and then change your mind a few seconds later.'

'No,' Zack smiled. 'I said I would get over it, not that I'd changed my mind. I'm not even sure if that's true. You're a very haunting young lady.'

'Like in nightmares, you mean?' she mocked.

'Nothing like nightmares,' his smile deepened, 'and you know it. Now eat your food and forget I ever mentioned it.'

That was much easier said than done, especially after the way she had reacted to him last weekend. But Zack did everything he could to make her feel at ease, chatting to her as if they were old friends as they ate their meal, almost making her forget the intimacy of those few moments before dinner. Almost . . .

'Thank you for a lovely evening——' she began.

'I'm sure they're expecting you to invite me in,' Zack interrupted her polite ending of the evening now that they were back outside the apartment.

'Then they'll be wrong, won't they?' she dismissed.

'Why?' He had turned to face her, his arm along the back of her seat.

'It's been a long day, I'd like to get to bed now,' she shrugged.

'You would prefer to kiss me goodnight out here?' He quirked blond brows.

Holly stiffened. 'I'd prefer not to kiss you goodnight anywhere!' she told him waspishly.

He gave a rueful shrug. 'The lights are still on in the lounge, which means someone has waited up for us.'

She instinctively looked up at the apartment, seeing the velvet curtains twitch back into place. 'Maxine?' she breathed softly, turning back to Zack.

'I would think so,' he nodded grimly. 'The journey probably tired James into going to bed hours ago.'

'Oh,' Holly sighed. 'So you think I should invite you in for coffee?'

'I think it might be a good idea.'

'Then you'd better come inside.' She climbed out of the sports car as best she could, feeling quite ruffled by the time she emerged out on to the pavement, although Zack seemed to suffer no such indignity, not even a hair out of place as he came round to join her. 'I wish you'd get yourself a decent car,' she snapped as they walked up the steps together to the entrance of the elegant building.

'Don't malign that car,' he gave her a pained look. 'I've had it longer than I care to remember.'

'I thought it seemed like the vehicle of a delinquent,' she took her bad humour at having to ask him in out on him.

Zack began to chuckle softly. 'Just for you I *might* change the car for something more—respectable.'

She gave him a sharp look, unsure whether or not he was serious or just mocking her. She decided it must be the latter. 'Your idea of respectable may not be the same as mine.' She let them into the apartment with the key James had given her earlier. 'In fact, I'm sure it isn't.'

'Probably not,' he agreed softly as they made their way to the lounge. 'But you could always come with me and help me choose it.'

'I don't think so,' she answered him in a pre-occupied voice, surprised to find the lounge empty now; whoever had watched them from the window— and she felt sure it had to have been Maxine—had now gone to bed. 'I doubt we would have the same taste, even in cars!'

Zack lounged back in an armchair. 'You might be surprised what we have in common. How about that coffee now?'

'Is it really necessary?' Holly looked pointedly at the room deserted of anyone but themselves.

'I very much doubt that Maxine will have fallen asleep just yet,' he drawled.

'You would be more familiar with her sleeping habits than I am!'

Her jibe wiped all humour from his face, and he sprang to his feet. 'Maybe I won't bother with the coffee after all.'

'Good. I——'

'But I'll take my kiss goodnight!' he rasped, pulling her towards him. 'Oh no, you don't, young lady!' He nimbly avoided the knee she was bringing up instinctively, knocking her off balance and down on to the sofa. 'I've been thinking about this all week,' he muttered as his head bent.

She was defeated before it began; she knew that she too had been waiting for this. She met his kiss with equal fervour, her arms up about his neck as she held him to her, the firmness of his body pressing down into her.

The dark grey dress she wore was in one of her usually demure styles, and yet Zack wasted no time in dispensing with the buttons, revealing her breasts with their fine covering of white lace, the dark brown nipples apparent through the lighter coloured material.

As she felt his lips against first one hardened tip through the sheer material, and then the other, she knew she longed for his more intimate caresses, that she didn't even want the lace bra between them, erotic as the sensation was. It seemed Zack didn't either; he was searching out the back fastening as he kissed her deep on the mouth.

'Holly, I—Oh!' Maxine's cold contempt as she entered the room and saw them together was like a slap on the face.

Zack swung his legs to the floor and sat up, effectively shielding Holly as she straightened her gown. 'Did you want something, Maxine?' he spoke in a calm voice.

The other woman seemed perfectly in control too, very beautiful in a light blue nightgown and négligé. 'I thought you'd already gone, and Holly seemed a long time going to bed; I wondered if anything was wrong.'

His mouth twisted at the deliberate fabrication. 'As you can see, it isn't.'

'No.' She tried to get another look at Holly as he still shielded her. 'I'll say goodnight, then.'

'Goodnight,' he nodded dismissively, watching with narrowed eyes as she left the room.

'How awful!' Holly at last gave rein to her feelings, burying her face in her hands.

'Maxine engineered the whole thing——'

'That doesn't make it any better!' she groaned.

Zack turned to her, leaning over her as she still lay full-length on the sofa. 'I wouldn't worry about it,' he advised gently. 'I've walked in on worse when she and James were going out together.'

'But this is me,' she shuddered her distaste. 'I don't do things like this!'

'Like what?' he frowned.

'Like—like letting comparative strangers make love to me on sofas,' she groaned, unable to look at him, sure he must despise her as much as she despised herself.

He smoothed the short red hair from her brow. 'I didn't make love to you, and we aren't strangers. I want you, and you want me, and we're both consenting adults. What Maxine or anyone else chooses to make of this is their affair. I want you, Holly.'

'But I—We're doing this for James.' She looked up at him with bewilderment.

'Not any more,' Zack shook his head. 'If we can help James and Maxine along the way then that's good, but as far as I'm concerned I'm now seeing you for myself.'

His gaze was intent. 'Maybe that sounds selfish, but that's the way you make me feel. I can't keep my hands off you!'

'You tricked me!' she accused dazedly.

He shook his head. 'I tricked myself, I had no idea it would turn out this way. Although I knew you'd cause me trouble the moment I looked into those violet eyes,' he added ruefully. 'I didn't know how right I was!'

Her composure was returning now. 'You aren't trying to tell me you're in love with me?' she scorned with contempt.

His mouth tightened. 'I'm telling you I'm attracted to you. Where that will lead us we'll just have to wait and see,' he shrugged.

'Maxine said it's usually as far as your bed,' mocked Holly, in control again.

'Sometimes it is——'

'Mostly,' she corrected.

'All right, mostly,' he ground out. 'But nothing about you has been usual since the moment we met, so I'm not expecting this to be either. What I do know is,' he added ruefully, 'that if you don't want to go to bed with me you're perfectly capable of making sure I get the message.'

'I certainly am,' she said sharply.

'Then what are you worried about?'

'I'm not——'

'Oh yes, you are.' Zack raised his brows. 'Perhaps you don't think you will say no.'

She knew she wouldn't; she was well aware of her own weakness that defeated all the self-defence classes she had taken during her last year at school. She was as attracted to Zack as he admitted being to her, and she didn't know what to do about it.

Zack was watching her closely, noting every emotion

flickering across her face. 'I think I should go now; you've had a long day. Is ten o'clock okay for the studio tomorrow?'

She was so taken aback by his decision to leave that she could only nod, only realising he had gone as her breath left her in a sigh. Zack had been difficult enough to cope with before, now that he had made his intentions clear towards her he would be impossible. And he had also made it clear that James was now secondary to his own desire for her, that she couldn't back out now if she wanted to.

The studio was exactly as she had imagined it would be, ultra-modern offices on the top floors, the actual recording studios on the lower floors.

'It all looks very complicated.' She tentatively touched the hundreds of control buttons on the instrument panel in the recording room, the studio beyond curiously quiet on this Saturday morning.

'It is,' grinned Zack, looking pleased with himself.

She gave him a curious look. 'Can you work this thing?'

He shrugged. 'I never ask anyone to do something I can't do myself. I can fill in for all the key jobs in the company, from tea-boy to this.' He touched the instrument panel almost lovingly, as if now that he was the executive he missed this close involvement with his recording stars.

'Tea-boy?' Holly teased him to break the moment of nostalgia, knowing herself that it never did any good to look back on the supposedly 'good times'.

He grinned, the moment passing. 'Of course. This place would fall apart without the tea and coffee that Ted provides.'

'And I thought this was a modern office, vending

machines included,' mocked Holly as they left the recording studio to go up to Zack's office.

'Vending machines?' he mused. 'You want vending machines, I'll show you vending machines.' He stopped the lift a couple of floors beneath his own, guiding her out into the corridor. 'Vending machines,' he dryly indicated the machines placed along one wall, all of them with 'Out of Order' notices on. 'They last an average of two days before we have to call in an engineer because they've broken down, hence Ted. If he breaks down we can easily replace him.'

Zack was a different man again in his own working environment, self-confident and assured, a man seriously dedicated to what he was doing, despite his casual appearance once again in faded denims and a fitted short-sleeved off-white shirt. Holly was having difficulty keeping up with the facets of this man.

His office bore more evidence of his pride in his profession—gold and platinum records on the walls, signed photographs from grateful artists who had been made into stars by this studio.

'It must be nice to be surrounded by your succeses.' Holly was amazed at the well-known names she could see as she slowly perused the photographs.

Zack grinned, his hands thrust into the back pockets of his denims. 'For every success story there's a hundred failures, but yes, I like what I do.'

She could tell that, she had been very aware of his pride as he showed her round, and she had to admit, to herself at least, that she was impressed. 'No Ted today?' She turned to look at him, a little thirsty after her morning looking round the studio.

'I told you, I can fill in for him if I have to,' he smiled. 'But I'm ready for lunch if you are.'

'Lunch? Oh, but——'

'It's after twelve,' he checked his watch to confirm this. 'And you aren't expected back.'

Holly gave him an irritated look. 'How do you know that?'

'Because I told Maxine you wouldn't be,' Zack dismissed with arrogance.

Holly sighed. 'I might have guessed. Okay, where are we going to eat?'

He raised dark blond brows. 'You're very amiable all of a sudden?' He sounded suspicious.

'About this, yes. I happen to be hungry,' she added mischievously.

'I should have known,' he said ruefully. 'Right, let's go. I'll take you to another of my favourite restaurants.'

She gave him an uncertain look. 'Neither of us is dressed to eat out.' Her own clothes, fitted trousers and a blue blouse, were as casual as his were.

'In this restaurant we are,' he told her mysteriously.

'A McDonald's!' she said disgustedly forty-five minutes later as they left the restaurant.

Zack eyed her teasingly. 'You enjoyed it, didn't you?'

Her mouth curved into a smile. 'It was delicious!'

'You may eat a lot,' he mocked, 'but at least this way you won't cost me a fortune. You're a cheap date, Holly Macey,' he taunted.

'Lucky for you I'm feeling all contented and full after my meal,' she pretended anger, really too satiated with good food to take offence at his remarks, 'otherwise I might be forced to retaliate.'

'The fact that you haven't tells me a lot.'

Holly flushed, stiffening slightly. 'That I like McDonald's?'

He shook his head. 'That you feel more relaxed with me. Now tonight——'

'Tonight?' She hadn't had time to correct him about

that last erroneous statement before he said something else that made her wary. 'I've spent most of the day with you, I'm not seeing you tonight too!'

'Of course you are,' he told her with ease. 'Who else would I take with me?'

'With you where?' She looked at him with suspicion.

'There's a promotional party I have to go to—well, actually I'm giving it, and——'

'No,' she cut in decisively, her mouth a stubborn line as she prepared to argue with him.

'Now don't be silly, Holly,' he cajoled. 'There'll only be a few people there——'

'A few *hundred*,' she snapped.

Zack sighed. 'All right, a few hundred. Don't tell me you're afraid of crowds?'

London crowds she was! The scandal that had been caused five years ago had been mainly confined to the family, but that wasn't to say she wouldn't one day meet someone who knew all the facts of her relationship with Alex. 'I don't happen to like London parties,' she amended.

'When did you last go to one?'

She flushed. 'That isn't the point——'

'How do they differ from other parties?'

'They just do,' she snapped.

'If you say so,' he said in a placating voice. 'But I'm committed into going.'

'That doesn't mean I have to go with you.'

Zack sighed at her stubbornness. 'I want you to,' he stated simply. 'We don't have to stay long, just so that I show my face for a few minutes.'

Holly blushed at his reminder that his interest in her was now very personal. 'I don't want to ruin the evening for you,' she said awkwardly.

'It will be ruined if you *don't* come with me.'

She had invited such an answer with her coy response, she realised that now, although Zack seemed perfectly sincere. 'We wouldn't stay long?' she repeated, knowing in that moment that she had once again weakened where this man was concerned. And he knew it too!

What to wear for that type of sophisticated party, that was the problem that faced Holly later. She had brought a couple of evening dresses with her because of last night, but neither the grey nor the black were really suitable, neither giving her the confidence she would need as Zack's companion for the evening.

She was grateful for the interruption of the knock on her bedroom door, although she became a little wary when Maxine walked into the room. She hadn't seen the other woman since last night, Maxine having her breakfast in bed this morning as usual, and Holly leaving the apartment before either James or Maxine had put in an appearance.

Maxine's brows rose at the two evening gowns lying across the bed. 'Going out?'

'Er—yes.' She felt even more uncomfortable than ever with the other woman. 'To a party, with Zack.'

'Of course.' Maxine pushed the black gown aside to sit on the side of the bed. 'Which one are you thinking of wearing' She looked critically at the gowns.

Holly grimaced. 'I can't decide.'

'No.' Maxine's tone of voice seemed to imply that there wasn't much to choose between them—that neither was very exciting!

But Holly already knew that, they had both been chosen for that very reason! 'Which would you suggest?' She stubbornly refused to be insulted.

Maxine shrugged uninterestedly. 'The black, I suppose, you wore the grey last night.'

'Hm.' She held it up in front of her, already knowing it did little for her.

Maxine obviously agreed with her. 'I'd lend you something of mine, but . . .' she trailed off pointedly.

Holly was well aware of the difference in their height and figures, and she didn't understand Zack's attraction to her if he had once been involved with Maxine, as he implied that he had. 'This gown will do,' she put it on a chair and hung the grey back in the wardrobe.

'If you're sure . . .' said Maxine in a bored voice.

She flushed at the deliberate slight. 'I'm sure,' she replied tightly. 'Now did you want me for something? Does James need me?' She hadn't seen her employer yet today either.

'Not that I know of,' the other woman dismissed. 'He hasn't left his room all day,' she added disgustedly. 'No, I came to see how your visit to the studio went.'

'Very well, thank you,' she answered stiffly.

'Good.' Maxine stood up, obviously not satisfied with that reply at all. 'I'll leave you to get ready for your evening out, I wouldn't want you to be late.'

A feeling of remorse washed over her. 'Er—What will you do this evening?' Surely Zack wouldn't mind if she invited his sister-in-law along?

The other woman looked at her with angry eyes. 'I do have other friends in London besides Zack,' she snapped.

'Of course—I'm sorry. I didn't mean——'

'I know exactly what you meant to do, Holly,' Maxine said vehemently. 'But I can assure you that I shall be far from lonely tonight. And once Zack has finished amusing himself with you he'll remember who his true friends are!'

'Maxine——'

'I have to go,' she rasped angrily. 'I'll be going out myself soon.'

Holly was shaking very badly by the time the door closed behind the other woman. She had only meant to be friendly by inviting Maxine to the party, sure Zack wouldn't mind just this once, but this scene with Maxine was reminiscent of scenes from the past. Then she had run away and left a wake of pain and confusion behind her, this time she would stick it out to the stubborn end.

Once again Zack was looking rakishly attractive when he called for her at eight-thirty, his green velvet jacket a perfect match for the darkness of his eyes, his shirt snowy white, his bow-tie the same velvet of his jacket, black trousers moulded to the lean length of his legs. Next to him Holly felt decidedly dowdy in the shapeless black dress, wishing she had chosen to wear the grey after all—at least that didn't make her look like a schoolmistress!

She welcomed Zack's comment of how beautiful she looked with scepticism. 'I think it's debatable which one of us looks more beautiful,' she told him dryly, fitting into the car with as much ease as he did tonight, while Zack drove competently at her side.

He laughed softly. 'It's nice to see you haven't lost that brittle sense of humour.'

Holly quirked auburn brows. 'Should I have done?'

He shrugged, the soft aroma of his aftershave tangy and pleasant to the senses. 'You're looking a little pale tonight, so I would guess at some sort of scene with Maxine.'

The incident with Maxine was only part of the trouble; it had been the memories of the past that had upset her the most. 'Not really a scene,' she dismissed. She just wondered how the visit to the studio had gone.'

'I'll bet she did!'

'She's confused, Zack,' sighed Holly. 'Angry with James for giving up when he has so much to fight for, angry with you for deserting her, and most of all angry with me because she thinks I've taken you from her.'

'I was never hers to take,' he said grimly.

'Never?' she prompted softly.

'I may have been once,' he dismissed with impatience. 'But that was years ago, before she married James.'

Holly felt inward relief at the knowledge. She had realised both brothers' interest in Maxine at some time, she just hadn't known quite where Zack fitted in, before or after James. It felt good to know that even then he had been loyal to his brother.

'I'll tell you about it some time,' he rasped now.

'I think I'd like that,' she said softly.

They were driving in the heart of London now, Zack parking his car behind a club that even Holly knew was 'the' place of the moment. She felt her nervousness grow as they approached the entrance, and was terrified of going inside.

'You look as if you're about to face the firing squad,' Zack chided at her pale appearance.

'I feel like it too,' she shuddered in reaction.

He looked genuinely concerned now. 'If you would rather not go . . .'

'No,' she shook her head firmly, 'I'll come with you.'

'Good girl!' He bent his head, his lips brushing across hers with butterfly softness. 'You have more colour now.' He gently touched her cheek.

'You might have more colour in one eye if you try that again,' she mocked.

His arm was firm about her waist as he held her to

his side. 'I knew you'd come back fighting,' he grinned.
'Okay, let's go in and face the mob.'

It was a glittering noisy party, everyone greeting
Zack by name, a number of people eyeing her curiously,
although Zack's air of possession where she was
concerned prevented any questions being asked directly.
She found during the next hour that beneath the glitter
and outrageous clothing some of the people were
normal human beings, that some of them were even
quite nice.

'I don't see Bobbie yet,' Zack muttered with a
frowning glance around the room.

'Bobbie?' she questioned above the loud music.

'Our supposed guest of honour. I might have known
she'd be late; Bobbie likes to make an entrance,' he said
dryly.

It was already after ten now; Holly wondered when
this 'entrance' was going to be! Although this was still
early by London standards, she knew that, it just
seemed to her that if the party was being given for the
other woman she could have at least turned up earlier
than this.

'If she doesn't soon put in an appearance she's going
to find she's the only one here,' Zack muttered angrily a
short time later, obviously losing patience with the
absent Bobbie.

Holly sipped the white wine which was all she had
had to drink all evening. 'I shouldn't worry about it too
much,' she consoled. 'The party seems to be going fine
without her.'

'That's the trouble,' he scowled. 'Where is the
damned girl?' he muttered. 'There are reporters here
who aren't going to wait for her much longer.'

'Reporters?' It hadn't occurred to her that any of this
glittering crowd were members of the press.

'You can hardly give a promotional party without publicity,' Zack explained impatiently.

'I suppose not. But I'm sure——'

'At last!' he breathed angrily, Holly forgotten, his gaze towards the door. 'Excuse me for a moment.' He looked down at her with hard eyes. 'I'm just going to tell our guest of honour how delighted I am she could allow us all a little of her time.'

His fury boded ill for the late Bobbie, another indication that he took his work very seriously. Nevertheless, Holly could feel a little pity for his unpunctual star, watching as he strode across the room with forceful movements. The young woman he greeted at the door was already surrounded by enthusiastic acquaintances, although they stepped aside to allow Zack through. No one would have been wise to argue with him at that moment, and they knew it.

Holly was given a clear view of their guest of honour as Zack joined the other woman, blonde hair streaked with silver that matched the glittering sheath of a dress that plunged almost to her navel in the front and yet covered her arms and back as completely as if she had been a nun. It was an outrageous dress, revealing that little, if anything, was worn beneath it, designed to make sure no one overlooked its wearer. And no one did! She was a really beautiful woman, slightly younger than Holly, she would think, her make-up darkly dramatic, her pouting mouth emphasised by the bright red lip-gloss.

There was something familiar about that mouth, something familiar about the whole sultry face and body. Bobbie . . .? Oh, dear God, not *Roberta*!

Holly watched Zack and the other woman as if in a dream now, barely aware of them coming towards her, of the way Bobbie clung to Zack's arm. But Zack seemed to have forgiven the other woman for her lateness now, his lazy smile firmly back in place as he spoke to the young girl at his side.

Brown eyes narrowed as the two women confronted each other for the first time in years, instant recognition flickering in their vindictive depths.

'Holly, I want you to meet my newest star, Bobbie Chance. Bobbie, this is a very good friend of mine, Holly Macey,' Zack made the introductions in complete ignorance of the tensison that reverberated between the two women.

'Holly,' Bobbie snapped tautly.

'Roberta,' Holly nodded warily.

The pouting red mouth twisted derisively. 'I haven't been called that since I was at school.'

'But that was when I knew you,' Holly reminded her stiffly.

'Yes,' Bobbie confirmed hardly. 'I hardly recognised you, Holly, you've changed.'

'So have you.'

'But for the better, I hope.' Her tone implied that that wasn't true of Holly.

She flushed at the intended insult. 'Of course.' She was as aware as Bobbie of how she had changed in the intervening years, how she had changed from a carefree young girl into a mature woman in a matter of days.

Zack was watching the two of them with puzzled eyes. 'You two actually know each other?'

'Oh yes,' Bobbie said hardly. 'Holly and I know each other very well.'

'But—how?' he frowned at this turn of events. 'Were the two of you at school together?'

'Among other things,' Bobbie drawled, a sudden spiteful mockery in her face as she looked at the stricken Holly.

She moistened stiff lips, desperate to stop Bobbie telling Zack the truth, and very much afraid the other woman was determined to do so. 'Bobbie——'

'Hasn't your "good friend" Holly told you that she broke up my father's marriage?' Bobbie cut in with sarcasm, obviously enjoying Holly's pained gasp of dismay.

Holly felt all colour leave her face, knowing as Zack turned to her with disbelieving eyes how guilty she must look to him. And she was.

CHAPTER SIX

HOLLY sat at Zack's side in numbed silence as they drove to his apartment; she had offered no resistance when he told her that was where he was taking her. After Bobbie's stark statement and her own apparent guilt she had known Zack would want to talk to her, in fact she didn't know how the two of them had stayed at the party for another hour after Bobbie left them to rejoin her enthusiastic crowd, both of them continuing to act normally in spite of all the unasked and unanswered questions that lay between them.

Zack's home was a typical bachelor apartment, kept neat and tidy by a daily cleaner, although the lounge bore marks of Zack's personality. A superior stereo system was set up in there, flanked by thousands of records and cassettes, and several more gold discs on the pastel-coloured walls.

But she wasn't there to admire the comfort of his home, and she sat down on the edge of one of the plush armchairs as she waited for him to finish the glass of brandy he had poured for himself as soon as they came in.

'Well?' he barked at last.

'Yes?' She eyed him warily, not liking his mood at all.

'Don't act coy, Holly,' he rasped, pale beneath his tan. 'Is what Bobbie accused you of true?'

'Zack——'

'*Is it?*' he demanded fiercely, his hands clasped into fists at his sides. 'You either did break up her father's marriage or you didn't.'

'It isn't as simple as that——'

'Of course it damn well is!' His eyes glittered furiously. 'Did you or didn't you?'

'Bobbie didn't know all the facts——'

'*Did you do it?*' he thundered.

Holly swallowed hard at the anger in him, moistening her lips. 'I did,' she admitted heavily. 'But——'

'My God!' Zack rasped. 'My God . . .' he muttered again, shaking his head disbelievingly.

'It wasn't as it sounds.' She looked up at him beseechingly. 'I didn't deliberately set out to break up the marriage.'

'But you did it anyway,' he said grimly, pouring himself some more brandy. 'I would never have believed it of you if you hadn't admitted it to me,' he spoke almost to himself.

'That's a lie,' Holly snapped. 'You were already convinced of my guilt before we even got here!'

'If you could have seen your face after Bobbie made the accusation you would have been convinced too!' he scorned.

She blushed at the truth of that. She had wanted to deny the truth of it after Bobbie had made the statement, but she couldn't do it. She had never intentionally hurt anyone in her life, and yet her involvement with Alex Chance had left a lot of people who were more than hurt, Bobbie being one of them. But not even to clear herself with Zack would she tell him the whole truth, because she was the one who had been hurt the most!

'Is this something you make a habit of?' Zack suddenly scorned harshly.

Holly looked stricken. 'What do you mean?'

His mouth twisted. 'Well, when I arrived on the scene

at James's house you seemed to be in the process of destroying his marriage too!'

'That isn't true!' she gasped.

'Did the man you were involved with at seventeen hurt you so much that you have to break up other relationships?' he demanded angrily. 'Bobbie's father and then James's?'

He had completely misunderstood what had happened in the past, although in the circumstances she couldn't altogether blame him for that. 'James's marriage was already in trouble, you know that,' she told him quietly. 'I agreed to help you try to save it.'

'So you did.' His mouth twisted with contempt. 'Why was that, I wonder? Could it be that you actually feel some remorse for destroying Bobbie's family and wanted to make amends when you found it was happening again with James?'

'You're twisting things——'

'Am I?' he scorned. 'I liked you, Holly, really liked you. Being told that you, of all people, are a marriage-wrecker is like being told there's no Father Christmas or tooth fairy all in one day!' He sighed. 'I just can't believe it of you.'

'Then don't,' she encouraged pleadingly.

'You've admitted it's true,' he reminded her heavily.

'In part, but you don't know the full story——'

'Then tell it to me,' he rasped, his face strained. 'Make me understand!'

She gave a choked sigh. 'I can't.'

'Why the hell not?'

She shrugged. 'I wasn't the only one involved——'

'I already gathered that,' he said disgustedly. 'Bobbie's father must have been willing, I realise that. But there isn't much difference between your own and Bobbie's ages, the man must have been old enough to be *your* father too.'

Holly was very pale now, almost grey. 'Yes, Bobbie's father was that.'

'Then why did you become involved with him?' Zack demanded. 'Don't tell me *that* was your infatuation with an older man?' he reminded her of the accusation he had once made to her concerning his brother.

'I——'

'Couldn't you have chosen someone who wasn't married, with children?' he snapped.

'I don't suppose it's occurred to you that I could have been the innocent one involved?'

'Were you?' His eyes narrowed.

'No,' she sighed. 'But I was young,' she defended herself. 'I didn't realise what I was getting myself into.'

'The man had a wife and child, you must have realised!' Zack shook his head, swallowing more of the brandy. 'It's going to take me a while to get used to your making a habit of being the "other woman" in broken marriages.'

Holly stood up agitatedly. 'I think I'd better go, before you become too insulting and say something we possibly both might regret.'

'Yes, perhaps you're right.' He ran a weary hand through the thickness of his hair. 'I need time to think about all this.'

'Could you call me a taxi?' she requested stiffly. 'I don't think you're in any condition to drive me back to the apartment.' He had been drinking at the party, and the brandy since he got here couldn't have helped his alcohol level at all. She had had to deal with the unpredictability of a drunken man once before, she didn't welcome the same scene with Zack.

'I'm not drunk——'

'A policeman might not agree with you,' she said dryly.

His jaw tightened. 'Admit it, you just don't want to be with me right now.'

Her head went back as she met the challenge in his words. 'That's right, I don't.'

'I'll call the taxi,' he told her abruptly.

Neither of them spoke as they waited for the taxi to arrive, Holly standing up stiffly to leave when the doorbell sounded. 'Thank you for tonight,' she told him curtly.

'Don't say you enjoyed yourself.' Zack came back from talking to the taxi-driver, his jacket and bow-tie discarded now that he wasn't going out again, the top two butons of his shirt undone. 'I don't think either of us have done that!'

Her mouth twisted. 'You didn't seem to be having too bad a time when you were with Bobbie,' she taunted.

'Don't start introducing stupid jealousies into this, Holly,' he snapped impatiently. 'We have enough problems between us already without that!'

She flushed at the deserved rebuke, not even sure why she had mentioned the younger woman. 'I'd better go——'

'Not yet.'

'The taxi-driver . . .'

'I asked him to wait downstairs. He's already been paid, so he'll wait,' he added arrogantly.

Her hands fluttered nervously. 'We have nothing more to say to each other tonight.'

'I disagree,' he bit out tautly. 'Oh, calm down, Holly,' he rasped as she glanced towards the door, as if ready to run at the slightest provocation. 'I'm not going to pounce on you, and you have your escape waiting downstairs. Before you go anywhere we'll clear up at least one misunderstanding between us. Bobbie is contracted to my studio, she's going to be a big star one day. I have no reason not to "have a good time" when I'm with her,' he derided. 'She's a charming child who simply likes the limelight.'

'She's almost my age,' Holly reminded him tautly.

'And yet there's a world of difference between you.'

'I should put that down to my chequered past,' she taunted hardly.

Zack looked more angry than ever. 'At any other time I might find your apparent jealousy towards Bobbie encouraging, right now I don't know what to think. Just understand that Bobbie Chance means nothing to me, that at the moment you hold all my attention. Now go if you must.'

'Zack——'

'God, why, Holly?' he groaned in despair as he pulled her into his arms, burying his face helplessly in her throat. 'Why did you have to do this to me?'

She was crushed so tightly in his arms she couldn't answer him, bent back across his arm as his lips travelled feveredly up her throat to her mouth. He forced her to his will, parting her mouth wide with his, the erotic movement more beseeching than the insult she had expected. Zack now believed, partly on her own admission, that she had had at least one affair with a married man, why should he now respect her? And yet he treated her with gentleness, savouring the taste of her mouth as his hands moved up to frame her face.

'Zack, I'm sorry,' she choked at the pain he was trying to convey to her. 'I'm so very sorry.'

'It doesn't matter, not now, not at this moment,' he moaned throatily, his eyes darkened to emerald. 'God, how I want you! Stay with me tonight, Holly. Stay here and let me love you.'

'I can't . . .' she refused, and even to her own ears she

didn't sound convincing. She couldn't want him to make love to her, she daren't let him come even that close!

'You can,' he encouraged heatedly. 'Don't you want me?' he frowned his hurt at the thought.

'It isn't that——'

'Then you do want me?' he pounced.

'I don't know. I'm confused.' She put a hand up to her temple. 'I have to go, Zack,' she pleaded.

He shook his head. 'Not when I want you so much.'

'Wanting me can't change what I did in the past, Zack.' She looked at him with pain in her eyes. 'I did break up Bobbie's father's marriage. They're divorced now, and all because of me.'

'If it hadn't been you it would have been someone else——'

'You can't dismiss it as easily as that,' she sighed wearily. 'And anyway, it wouldn't be true.'

'If a man can stray once then he'll do it again.'

'You don't understand——'

'Because you won't let me,' he ground out fiercely. 'Because you won't tell me what happened.'

'No,' she acknowledged flatly.

'Then go,' he turned away. 'Just go.'

She wanted to run to him at that moment, to tell him all that had happened. But she couldn't do it, the pain went too deep even to tell Zack the whole truth. It went too deep for her to face at times, which was why she did her best not to think about it for the majority of the time.

'I'll be over to see you tomorrow.' Zack's words stopped her at the door.

'There's no need——'

'There's every need, damn you!' His eyes glittered. '*I* need! I care about you too much to part like this. I'll see you tomorrow afternoon before you leave.'

She swallowed hard, nodding slowly. 'All right,' she agreed softly. 'Although nothing will have changed by then.'

'*I* might have,' he ground out.

She was no nearer to understanding Zack now than she had been when they first met. He acted as if he were actually hurt by her reluctance to confide in him about the past, but to do that he really would have to feel something for her. He said he cared about her, but what did that mean?

The taxi reached James and Maxine's apartment all too quickly for her, thoughts whirling round and round in her head, all of them without answers. Luckily there was no one up tonight to see her confusion, and she escaped quickly to her bedroom, to the privacy of her thoughts.

To match her mood of depression it was raining the next morning, and when James asked if she would mind working for a few hours she readily agreed, needing something to take her mind off her meeting with Zack this afternoon.

She had slept badly, the dark bruises beneath her eyes evidence of that, something Maxine was quick to remark upon once James had left the dining-room to prepare his work, leaving Holly and his wife still eating. Holly felt sure the other woman's unusual appearance at the breakfast-table this morning was not accidental.

'You aren't looking well,' Maxine drawled bluntly.

'The noise from the traffic kept me awake last night,' she evaded.

'Really?' the other woman derided. 'I don't recall there being much traffic, and certainly not Zack's car,' she added pointedly.

Too late Holly once again realised how easily she had

played into the other woman's hands. 'He didn't drive me home last night,' she revealed stiffly. 'I took a taxi.'

'Really?' Maxine drawled again.

'Yes,' she snapped. 'It was late, he'd been drinking at the party, and I—I thought it best if he didn't drive.'

'How odd,' the other woman mocked. 'I've never known Zack to be over the limit before.'

'I doubt that he was last night,' she said sharply. 'I just didn't want him to take the risk.'

'And what did Zack think?' She arched dark brows.

Holly flushed at the taunt. 'He agreed with me,' she bit out resentfully.

'I see.' Maxine obviously 'saw' only what she wanted to see, standing up. 'Well, you mustn't feel too badly about it, I did warn you he wouldn't stay amused for long.'

'It wasn't like that——'

'It's all right, Holly,' she placated. 'But perhaps in future you will listen to me when I try to offer you advice.'

She hated Maxine's patronising tone, would have liked to wipe that self-satisfied smile off the beautiful face. But she and Zack had started out seeing each other only because of James, and after last night she had a feeling Zack's interest in her really would be over. Better to let Maxine have her gloat now and get it over with!

James seemed in no hurry to begin work when she joined him, and he looked more strained than she had ever seen him. Her relationship with Zack was taking its toll on everyone!

'Did you have a good time yesterday?' James finally asked, gruffly.

'Yesterday . . .?'

'At Zack's studio,' he prompted.

She had forgotten all about the visit to the recording studio after meeting Bobbie last night. 'It was very interesting,' she nodded, relaxing a little in his company.

His mouth twisted. 'Maxine has always found it very annoying that Zack refuses to take her there.'

'Oh.' She didn't know what else to say!

'He must be very attracted to you.'

Holly blushed. 'I wouldn't say that——'

'I would.' His hand covered hers. 'If he's really serious about you then I wish you both luck,' he said with obvious sincerity.

Now she really was at a loss for words. The last thing she had expected was for her and Zack to get James's blessing! So much for their plan, they had completely misjudged James's reaction.

'I don't know how we feel,' she evaded questioning hazel eyes. 'Would you like to start work now?'

'If you would,' he nodded slowly, still looking at her.

He was inviting her confidences about Zack and herself, and she just didn't know what to say to him. Your brother and I started seeing each other just to make you jealous and it backfired on us? She doubted he would appreciate the truth of that—and she couldn't blame him!

'I think so,' she agreed briskly. 'That is why we're in here, after all,' she added brightly.

'Holly——'

'I must have a lot to catch up on,' she continued as if he hadn't spoken. 'You've been working ever since we arrived on Friday.'

'Not all the time,' he said grimly. 'London has an unsettling effect on me. I'll be glad to return to Hampshire.'

Holly heartily seconded that. But she had to get

through her meeting with Zack this afternoon first, and she wasn't looking forward to it at all. Last night Zack had been angry, too angry to think straight, and the drink hadn't helped either. But today would be a different matter, and she knew what a sharp mind he had normally. Maybe he would even manage to get the whole truth out of her!

When he arrived shortly after two o'clock he didn't look as he had slept any better than she had, his expression grim, a tense look about his mouth. He was wearing fitted light green trousers and a dark green shirt, the latter partly unbuttoned down his chest, the sleeves turned back to just below his elbows. He looked lithe and attractive, and potentially dangerous!

'We're going for a drive,' he announced in a voice that brooked no argument.

Nevertheless, Holly offered one! 'We're leaving in a couple of hours.'

'I'll have you back by then,' he promised abruptly. 'Unless you would like to talk here?' He derided the fact that they had already been interrupted twice, once by an irate Maxine that he should be here to see Holly, and another time by a maid enquiring if they would like tea or coffee brought to them.

'A drive would be nice,' she agreed curtly.

Zack didn't drive far, just away from the noise and traffic of London, turning off down a quiet country road that looked as if it hadn't seen a car in years, parking a short distance off the road.

'You certainly know some spots,' Holly told him lightly. 'Another of the places you used to visit as a child?'

'I've never been here before,' he dismissed. 'Shall we walk?' he suggested.

'Why not?' She continued to try and keep the conversation light.

They walked silently side by side, not touching, but not physically distant either, although mentally it was a different matter. Zack was worlds away from her, very deep in thought, his hands thrust into his denims pockets, his shoulders hunched over dejectedly.

'I've thought about things a lot since last night,' he said suddenly, not looking at her. 'Hell, I've done nothing else,' he scowled.

'And?'

'I've come to no conclusions.' He did look at her now, his eyes bitter. 'I never expected, or wanted, you to be a paragon,' he rasped. 'But hearing you admit to breaking up a man's family means you aren't the woman I thought you were either.'

'Zack, you're talking as if I've betrayed *you*,' she interrupted gently.

'And haven't you?'

She paled. 'Of course not,' she answered tremulously. 'We don't love each other, we don't even like each other very much—we're just attracted to each other. And I've never demanded an explanation about Maxine from you. Surely I would have done if I felt anything deeper for you than attraction?' she reasoned.

'You were never in a mood to listen about Maxine,' he reminded her gratingly. 'You were always too busy throwing out accusations to listen to me.'

'As you're doing now?'

'With a difference. I've never admitted that Maxine has ever meant more to me than a sister-in-law since she married James,' he said grimly.

'It doesn't really matter what you've admitted,' she dismissed. 'As I've already said, I've never asked for the explanations.' She had trusted him without the need for words, something he didn't seem capable of doing where she was concerned!

'Well, you're going to get them, whether you want them or not!' He stared sightlessly in front of him. 'We'll clear up *all* the misunderstandings between us today.'

'Except my involvement with Bobbie's family.'

'That too,' he ground out.

'No,' she shook her head firmly.

Zack gave her a furious glare before turning away. 'I knew Maxine first,' he began. 'She was my girl-friend when she met James. I could see she liked him, but I wasn't serious about her, although I did like her, a lot. I still do, but in a different way. At first James had little time for her, completely engrossed in his career, and then Maxine would use me to try and make him take notice of her. I didn't mind,' he smiled at the memory. 'In fact, I found it quite amusing. Poor James was caught and he didn't even know it! Even when he did realise it and actually proposed he kept her hanging about for years before he married her. Patience has never been one of Maxine's virtues, and periodically she would get me to take her out in order to make James jealous. It usually worked too.'

'Which is why you thought it would after his accident,' she realised.

His mouth twisted. 'We underestimated him that time, although Maxine began to actually believe in it, began to think she really was in love with me.'

'So you've never loved her?'

'No!'

Holly hadn't known she could feel so relieved, and about such a subject. She had pieced together bits of the past from other things Zack had told her, but it was nice to know it all. Although it didn't help them now!

She would never be able to redeem herself in Zack's eyes.

'Our plan to help James hasn't worked this time either,' she told him softly. 'He told me this morning that he approves of us seeing each other.'

'That's a reversal of attitude,' Zack scowled.

'I think we just misunderstood his feelings towards me, that he was only being protective.'

'No,' Zack said firmly. 'He was leading up to more than that.'

She shrugged. 'And now he thinks we're serious about each other.'

His mouth was tight. 'He's an incurable romantic,' he mocked harshly.

It wasn't something she would ever have accused James of, his books were often rawly graphic, but she didn't dispute the fact. 'I think we should be getting back now. I still have a few things to pack, and I won't make myself any more popular if I'm late.'

'We haven't settled a thing!'

'I told you last night,' she reminded him softly, 'there's nothing to settle. We don't need to even see each other again now that James has accepted the relationship, there's no reason to.'

'You know that isn't true.' He shook her gently by the shoulders. 'I care for you, Holly, really care for you.'

'It's no use——'

'Holly, *please*!' he groaned as he bent to kiss her, a gently pleading kiss that asked for her response to him this one last time.

She clung to him, her body arched into the hardness of his, her thin silk dress scant barrier between their two bodies. But it was still too much for Zack, and his thighs moved against her restlessly, throbbing with a desire he didn't try to hide.

She made no protest as the zip to her dress was slowly moved down her spine, quivering with reaction as she felt the warmth of Zack's hands against the dampness of her skin, the dress falling unheeded to her waist, the pink lace bra cut low over her breasts, the dusky nipples visible through the sheer material.

With one deft movement Zack had unfastened the bra and thrown it to the ground at their feet, one lean hand curling about her bared breast, the weight of it fitting snugly into the palm.

None of their previous lovemaking had prepared her for this, for the trembling ecstasy that flooded her body as Zack's thumbtip flicked across the hardened nipple.

'Beautiful.' He bent to caress the hardened peak with his lips and tongue, his hair like pure gold against her pale skin. 'You're so beautiful, Holly.' His attention passed to the other nipple as he held her into him, one of his hands caressing her hip beneath her dress.

She wanted more than just his caress, moving impatiently against his hand, sighing her pleasure as deft fingers moved beneath the lace of her panties. She was on fire with wanting him, needing his fierce possession, she had waited so long for a man to touch her again in this way.

'Take your clothes off, Zack,' she encouraged urgently, pulling at his shirt, baring his chest to remove the garment altogether, kissing him with a heated passion that demanded he make her his, here and now. 'Zack, Zack . . .!' she groaned weakly. 'I'm ready for you now, Zack,' she whimpered. 'Please, please . . .'

'It's all right, darling. It's all right,' he assured her raggedly as she shuddered in his arms. 'Let me get the blanket from the car, and then——'

'Don't leave me!' She clung to him, mindless in her

need for him. 'I don't need the blanket, I just want you.'

'And God knows I want you!' He lowered her quickly to the ground, his eyes fiercely dark as he removed the rest of her clothes before shaking off his own.

He was beautiful in his nakedness. Holly had never seen a man who was so beautiful, his skin a healthy golden colour, not an ounce of superfluous flesh on him anywhere, his thighs powerful in their full arousal.

Holly moved to caress him with fierce tenderness, to kiss him to the mindless pleasure he didn't quite share yet, knowing as he collapsed on his knees at her side that he couldn't hold back any longer. And she didn't want him to, she had been waiting for his possession for too long, it seemed.

The hardness of him inside her was an intrusion that made her gasp, and then sigh as each thrust brought new pleasure, his movements slow inside her as he caressed her breast with the moist warmth of the tip of his tongue.

The taut caress of his thighs was becoming too much for her as his mouth returned to hers, his hands firm on her bottom. The passion spiralled out of control, Holly aware of Zack's own cries of pleasure as she reached a shuddering climax of ecstasy so strong she felt faint with the release of it.

Zack collapsed above her, his face buried in her throat as he continued to tell her how beautiful she was, how much he still wanted her.

But with the physical release came the realisation of what she had done, how she had begged him to make love to her. It was what she had always feared happening, what she had always known could happen and had guarded against all these years. Today her guard her slipped irrevocably.

Zack looked down at her with a tender smile, sensing none of her inner turmoil. 'That was the most beautiful experience of my life,' he told her softly.

She turned away. 'Could you let me up, Zack? I—My back is getting sore.'

'Of course.' He gently removed himself from her body, both of them shuddering at the spasm of pleasure such a move evoked on their sensitive flesh. 'You should have let me get the blanket after all,' he teased as he saw the criss-cross marks of the grass on her back.

She quickly pulled on her clothes, unable to look at him. 'Yes,' she answered dully.

'There's no rush, Holly,' he assured her softly. 'We're quite alone here.'

'I—I feel better with my clothes on,' she evaded his hands as he reached for her.

'Holly . . .?'

'Shouldn't you be getting dressed too?' she suggested brittlely.

'Holly, what is it?' he frowned. 'Darling, tell me what's wrong? I know we didn't plan on making love, but it was the most beautiful thing imaginable, so tell me what's wrong'

She still couldn't look at him, filled with shame for what she had done. 'Could you get your clothes on first?'

'You didn't say that a moment ago!'

She flushed at his angry taunt. 'Please,' she said huskily, knowing by the sound of his movements that he was indeed dressing.

'Now,' he barked grimly, 'what the hell is the matter? Talk to me!'

Holly turned to face him, finding him fully dressed now, his expression harsh in his confusion. She knew it was his hurt that was making him angry with her, and yet she could do nothing to help him, was too busy trying to keep herself from falling apart. 'This—what just happened, it changes nothing between us,' she told him stiltedly.

'It changes everything.'

'No,' she shook her head. 'It should never have happened.'

'But it did. And at your instigation, I might add,' he rasped.

She flushed. 'Yes,' she could only admit the truth of that. 'But it didn't mean anything, don't you see? I thought I cared for Alex once too, but it was only physical curiosity.'

'Are you saying that's all this was?' Zack asked disbelievingly.

'Yes,' she choked.

'I don't believe you!'

'It's true.' She swallowed hard. 'A man isn't the only one to feel the curiosity of knowing how a person makes loves. I felt that curiosity with Alex once, and now with you.'

'You can't mean this,' Zack shook his head.

'I do,' she nodded unflinchingly.

'But—Are you saying you feel nothing for me?'

'Nothing,' she confirmed dully.

'But you made love to me as if you cared,' he persisted.

'We didn't make love at all, Zack,' she spoke softly. 'We had sex. We *wanted* each other.'

He shook his head dazedly. 'I don't really know you at all, do I?'

'No,' Holly shook her head.

'Let's get back to town,' he rasped. 'The air here is suddenly too stale for me to breathe.'

She knew he was hurt, but she owed him the truth

about what had happened. She had fought her
sensuality since that time with Alex, but Zack's
persistent wearing down of her barriers from the
moment they had met had been effective; it had been
inevitable that this should one day happen. She wished
as deeply as Zack that it hadn't; she had never wanted
to know that weakness again.

CHAPTER SEVEN

HAMPSHIRE was very lovely this time of year, very hot too. James spent a lot of time working out in the garden now that they were back. For Holly it had been a very long week, when she had done so much soul-searching she felt ill from lack of sleep. Alex had called her a wanton, among other things, and surely her behaviour with Zack only confirmed that. And yet she missed him as she had never missed Alex, missed his company more than she had thought possible, and wondered what he had been doing since they had parted so abruptly last weekend.

She had told him she didn't want to see him again, and after what had happened she knew she wouldn't. Zack had as much pride as the next man!

But she was finding it difficult to settle down again in Hampshire; she was restless and impatient, daily swims in the pool adjoining the house not helping to ease her tension at all. In fact, she couldn't ever remember feeling this restless before.

By the end of the week she knew she was ready for a change, that the quiet tranquillity here that had once so appealed to her now no longer satisfied her. Besides, this was Zack's brother's home, and the fact that she was living here could now stop him visiting James.

James greeted the news of her wanting to leave with frowning displeasure. 'I thought you were happy here?'

'I was—I am,' she amended quickly. 'I just—I need a change.'

'Perhaps a few weeks off,' he suggested. 'We've been

working hard the last few months, perhaps you just
need a holiday.'

'No. I need a complete change,' she said adamantly.

He sighed his impatience. 'It's Zack, isn't it? He's
hurt you after all.'

'No——'

'He has,' James insisted softly. 'I knew he would, but
I'd hoped that with you—But this doesn't mean you
have to leave here,' he said sharply. 'Zack comes here
very rarely now, and you could always take a few days
off when he's coming to visit if it would make you feel
more comfortable.'

Holly shook her head. 'It wouldn't work, James. And
my wanting to leave has nothing to do with Zack.
Maybe it was the weekend in London that did it,' she
invented lightly. 'But I've found that I miss those
famous "bright lights".'

'But you told me you hadn't lived in London for
years,' he frowned.

'I've lived in other towns, though,' she shrugged.

He drew in a ragged breath. 'I suppose, if you would
be happier there, we could all move to London.'

Her eyes widened. Before, James had always rejected
any suggestion that they go to London, in fact only last
weekend he had claimed it had an unsettling effect on
him. At the time she hadn't questioned the meaning of
that statement, but now she did. She had taken it to
mean that he couldn't work there, but it could also have
meant that it reminded him too much of the life he used
to lead, before the accident.

'You once told me you could never go back there to
live,' she said.

His hand moved to clasp hers as she sat in the chair
beside him. 'I could stand the move if it would make
you happy.'

'Me? But——'

'You must know how fond I am of you, Holly. I tried to tell you that weekend Zack came to stay, and then I got sidetracked by your interest in each other. But if it's all over between the two of you ...?'

'It is. But——'

'We could have a good life together, Holly,' he persisted. 'I know a husband in a wheelchair may not——'

'Husband?' she repeated incredulously, sure she must have misheard him.

'I want to marry you,' he told her quietly.

She shook her head. 'But you're already married,' she gasped. 'To Maxine.'

'We can be divorced——'

'Have you spoken to her about that?' Holly frowned.

'I don't need to,' he said grimly. 'It's pretty obvious that she's no longer happy here with me, that she and Zack have been seeing each other in London for years.'

'That isn't true,' she defended heatedly. 'Not in the way you mean, anyway.'

James eyes narrowed. 'And what do you know about it?'

'Zack told me——'

'Zack!' he echoed derisively. 'Of course he would deny it—you were hardly likely to go out with him if you thought he was having an affair with Maxine.'

'And what reason would she have for allowing him to see me if they *are* having an affair?'

His mouth was tight. 'She's always been very gullible where Zack is concerned, she'll forgive him anything.'

'How can you talk about them like this?' Holly frowned. 'And last weekend you told me you approved of my seeing your brother!'

'What else could I say?' James shrugged. 'I didn't

want to alienate you from me. Besides, warning you off him didn't seem to be working.'

She gave an impatient sigh. 'Neither did encouraging me to see him.'

'It didn't?' He quirked blond brows. 'But it's all over between you now,' he pointed out.

'And it was my decision,' she nodded.

'Yours?' He looked startled. 'But I thought——'

'Yes?'

'Zack has a reputation for brief affairs,' he flushed at her obvious anger.

'And you thought I was going to be another of them.' Her mouth twisted derisively. 'I'm sorry to disappoint you, James.'

'I'm not disappointed. You could never disappoint me, Holly.' His hand tightened on hers. 'Let's forget about Zack and concentrate on us. As I was saying, I realise a husband in a wheelchair isn't what you probably had in mind for your future, but just because I can't walk it doesn't mean I'm incapable of making love to you.'

'Then why haven't you made love to Maxine since your accident?'

His face darkened angrily. 'Who told you that?' His mouth firmed. 'Zack, of course.' He removed his hand from hers. 'What else has he told you about me?' He turned away.

'That there's no reason why you shouldn't be walking.'

'Oh no?' he said bitterly. 'Then why am I still in this damned wheelchair?'

Holly shrugged. 'I was hoping you might be able to explain that.'

He swung his chair away from her to stare out of the window, the weather was cloudy and the bay was not visible to him today. 'I can't walk,' he told her flatly.

'Have you tried?'

'I can't even stand up!'

'Oh, James!' She went to sit at his feet, her hands over his clenched ones. 'You can't expect to be able to just get up and walk—you need help for that, professional help.'

'A psychiatrist?'

'Don't be silly,' she shook her head frowningly. 'I was thinking more of a physiotherapist.'

'But if it's all in my head, as they say it is——'

'That doesn't mean you're insane,' she chided gently. 'Your brain just rejects the idea of walking because you're sure you can't do it.'

'I'm afraid there's more to it than that,' he sighed, not looking at her.

'Tell me,' Holly encouraged.

James gave a self-derisive smile. 'You're going to think me very stupid after I just asked you to marry me.'

'Fondness isn't love, so I'll forget you ever mentioned it,' she promised instantly.

His expression was mocking. 'I wish you didn't sound so eager when you said that.'

'James . . .!' She squeezed his hand encouragingly.

'It's all right,' he shrugged dismissively, one hand moving to massage his brow. 'I don't think I know what I'm doing any more. Will you forgive me for embarrassing you just now? I don't know why I would think you were even interested in marrying someone like me when——'

'If it weren't for Maxine perhaps I might have been,' she consoled. 'But she's the person you really love.'

'I did——'

'You still do,' Holly insisted, knowing it to be the truth.

'Maybe, but I hate her a little too. You asked why I haven't made love to her, the answer is simple—I'm afraid to try. Can you imagine the indignity of it all?' he groaned.

'I'm sure she would never have found it that way.'

'Wouldn't she? After the accident, when they told me I would be in a wheelchair, I *begged* her to divorce me. She wouldn't hear of it, and after a while, when the worst of the shock had worn off, I was glad she wouldn't. But I've come to realise it was only pity that made her stay——'

'I'm sure you're wrong about that,' Holly cut in frowningly.

'No,' he shook his head. 'How could she still love me, a cripple, half a man? She had to have stayed because she felt sorry for me. When I realised that I began to build my life without her, I had my new career, Robert to take care of all my needs, I no longer needed a wife. And yet still she stayed, her sense of loyalty making her do so. And then I realised I still loved her, despite her frequent trips to London, and I began to fear that she might leave me after all, that I'd driven her away. So I accepted the trips to London, even though it soon became obvious it was Zack she was seeing there,' he added bitterly.

'But only as a friend,' Holly insisted. 'Please believe that.'

'It's difficult——'

'So has Maxine's life been the last two years.' She looked pleadingly into his eyes, willing him to understand how his wife must have felt all this time. 'She was as shocked as you were by the accident, and yet you immediately rejected her. The fact that you later accepted she was staying can't have healed the wound that must have caused, especially as you shut her out physically too. You no longer needed her, in any way, made her feel superfluous. She must love you very much to have put up with your treatment of her.' Strangely, Holly now realised this to be true, understood all that Zack had been trying to explain to her, even understood why in the end Maxine had tried to turn to him for the affection her husband denied her.

'I don't know how she feels any more, she never talks to me about it,' James said dully. 'I want to walk again, Holly, but if I did Maxine would no longer have a reason to stay.' He looked at her with tortured eyes.

'You're wrong,' she choked at the misunderstandings that were driving these two people apart. 'She wants to stay, to show you how much she loves you, but she's frightened of your rejection again. She's a very strong-willed person, James, she could help you enormously if you'd only let her.'

'It may be too late for that.'

'It isn't,' Holly said with certainty. 'And I wouldn't have made you a very good wife at all,' she teased him. 'I would have let you continue just as you are.'

'I know.'

She sat up on her knees. 'And it isn't what you need or really want, James,' she told him gently. 'I think it's high time you and Maxine sorted out your differences.'

He shook his head. 'I have no idea how to go about it. She's grown hard the last few months, brittle, as if she no longer cares about anything, least of all me.'

'She cares,' Holly assured him. 'Although after the way you've treated her lately she might need a little convincing of that!'

'Will you still be leaving?' He gave her a concerned look. 'I can assure you, even if Maxine and I don't sort out our problems, that I'll never embarrass you by mentioning marriage between us again.'

She smiled. 'I might want you to if I stayed,' she teased gently.

'You're a very kind person, Holly,' he touched her cheeks gently. 'I'm sorry things haven't worked out for you here.'

'So am I.' Her expression was shadowed now. 'But I really do have to leave, straight away if possible?'

He nodded. 'I'll miss you,' he sighed.

'I'll miss you too.' She moved up to kiss him warmly on the cheek, gasping a little as he turned sideways and captured her mouth with his. But it was only a pleasant kiss of one friend to another, no passion involved on either side.

'What on earth is going on here?' gasped a furiously incredulous voice.

The two of them sprang guiltily apart, although in reality they had nothing to feel guilty about. But the accusation in Maxine's face was enough to make Holly's blood run cold, and James looked as stricken. So much for him wanting to divorce Maxine and marry her—the poor man was as confused about what he wanted as his wife was!

Holly stood up, smoothing the skirt of her navy blue dress. 'This isn't as it looks——'

'No?' Maxine looked at her with angry eyes. 'Not content with flirting with Zack, you now have to try your seemingly recently discovered feminine wiles on my husband too!'

'I didn't flirt with Zack——'

'Or James?' Maxine snapped.

'Maxine——'

'I wish I could say it's nice to know you're interested in women again, James,' Maxine spat the words at him.

'But you had no right!' Tears glistened in her eyes. 'I can hardly believe this.' She began to crumble before their eyes, her face a picture of misery and pain. 'I'm going to London for a while, James,' she told him shakily. 'And I'm not sure if I'll be back. You know where to reach me if you have—have anything to say to me.'

'Maxine——'

'Excuse me,' once again she interrupted him, turning on her heel and hurrying from the room.

'Oh *God!*' James buried his face in his hands.

'I'll talk to her——' Holly began.

'I doubt if she'll listen,' he shook his head. 'Not after this.'

'I'll *make* her listen,' Holly told him fiercely. 'God, but you're a stubborn, bullheaded family!'

He gave a humourless smile. 'Including Zack?'

'Mainly Zack,' she snapped, hurrying after Maxine.

It wasn't difficult to find the other woman; she was in her bedroom packing, the tears streaming down her face hindering her vision. She stiffened as Holly knocked on the open bedroom door, turning sharply to glare at her. 'What do you want?' she asked ungraciously.

'To explain——'

'What you were doing kissing my husband?' Maxine threw more clothes haphazardly into the suitcase. 'It was perfectly obvious what you were doing.'

'I doubt it,' Holly sighed.

'Oh, but it was,' Maxine rasped. 'How long has this been going on between the two of you?'

'It hasn't——'

'You mean this was the first time you've kissed each other?' she scorned. 'I admit that was what I thought at the time, but I must have been being incredibly naïve.

God, the two of you spent so much time alone together, and I never suspected a thing!'

'There was nothing to suspect——'

'Don't lie, Holly,' Maxine bit out between clenched teeth. 'I saw the two of you with my own eyes. I don't think I would ever have believed it if I hadn't!' she said self-derisively. 'For two long years he's been a physical non-participant in our marriage, and within months of your coming here all that's changed. But it's no longer me he desires!'

'He certainly doesn't desire me,' Holly sighed. 'What you saw was an emotionally charged kiss——'

'I could see that!'

'—due to the fact that I'd just told James I'm leaving, immediately,' she finished pointedly.

Maxine gave her a startled look. 'You're *what?*'

'I'm leaving,' she repeated. 'As soon as I can.'

'But I—Why?' all the anger seemed to have gone out of the other woman now.

'I think you can guess why.'

'James——'

'No, not James.' Holly met Maxine's gaze steadily, willing her to understand.

'Zack . . .' she breathed softly.

'Partly,' Holly nodded. 'Although that isn't really important right now; what matters is that you should go and talk to James.'

Maxine sat down heavily on the bed. 'I don't know what to say to him.'

'I think it's more a question of what he wants to say to you,' Holly explained gently.

The other woman gave her a startled look. 'Say to me?' she repeated dazedly. 'What do you mean?'

'Go and talk to him,' she encouraged. 'He's waiting for you in the study.'

'He is?'

'Yes,' nodded Holly.

Maxine stood up, moving to the adjoining bathroom to check her appearance. 'God, I look a mess!' she groaned, scrubbing the streaked make-up from her face.

'I don't think James will notice,' Holly assured her softly.

The other woman looked younger and much more vulnerable without the perfect make-up she habitually wore. 'He's always liked to see me looking my best——'

'You never look anything else to him,' Holly told her. 'Now go and talk to him, stop the worrying he's going through at the moment.'

Maxine hesitated at the door. 'He isn't going to ask me to leave?' she asked tremulously.

'Far from it,' Holly smiled. 'He's been a little confused, I think you both have the last few months.' She watched the other woman blush as she knew Holly spoke of her imagined feelings for Zack. 'But he's realised now that it's you he really loves. I believe you love him too?'

'Yes . . .'

'Then what are you waiting for?' Holly chided teasingly.

'Holly, about the things I said earlier——'

'Forgotten.'

'And the way I've been so mean to you about Zack——'

'That's forgotten too,' Holly told her briskly.

Still Maxine stood at the door. 'I've misjudged you, Holly,' she said slowly. 'I think, if we'd given ourselves the chance, that we might even have been friends in time.'

'Probably,' she agreed.

One thing Holly had learnt in the last few minutes—

she didn't respond to every man who kissed her. James's mouth on hers hadn't been unpleasant, but it certainly hadn't induced any passion either. So what did that make of the accusation Alex had once thrown at her about how she had the sort of fiery sensuality that any man could enjoy? Did that mean she had responded to Zack as just another man or as one she really cared about? She didn't have time to puzzle her answer as Maxine's ear-splitting scream filled the house.

Holly ran down the stairs so fast she almost fell in her haste, understanding the reason for Maxine's near-hysteria as soon as she reached the study. James lay unconscious on the floor!

Maxine was on her knees beside him, her face paper-white. 'What shall I do? What shall I do?' She turned to Holly in a panic.

'Call a doctor,' Holly instructed briskly. 'I'll get Robert to carry him upstairs.'

'Are you sure we should move him?'

James looked so still she didn't know what to think. 'I'm not sure of anything, but we can't just leave him lying there.'

'I suppose not,' Maxine agreed reluctantly.

'The doctor,' Holly prompted again as the other woman seemed almost paralysed herself.

'Oh—oh yes.' She stood up, still looking anxiously at James. 'I don't understand how it happened,' she muttered almost to herself.

'Neither do I,' Holly told her gently. 'But one thing I do know, James was sitting in his chair near the window when I left him.'

Both women looked at the chair that still stood in front of the window, James now lying several feet away from it in the middle of the room.

Maxine looked at her with excitement in her eyes. 'You don't think——'

'We mustn't jump to conclusions, Maxine,' warned Holly, although she had to admit to feeling a certain amount of excitement herself. If James *had* attempted to walk then he might have made those first tentative steps that would be the beginning of his complete recovery. 'Ah, Robert,' she turned to him as he appeared in the doorway, also summoned by Maxine's scream. 'Could you get Mr Benedict up to his room, please. Maxine, the doctor,' she prompted again, more firmly this time.

James had recovered consciousness by the time the doctor arrived, although he would say little. The two women sat in the lounge as the doctor made his examination.

'I hardly dare hope.' Maxine sipped at the reviving tea Holly had ordered for them both.

'Then don't,' Holly advised gently. 'We could be wrong.'

The blue eyes glowed. 'But what if we're right, what if he did try and walk?'

'Don't you think we should wait for the doctor's verdict before you start making plans?'

'I suppose so,' she acknowedged reluctantly, although the air of excitement remained with her.

Holly hardly dared hope herself, although it looked promising. Surely there was no other way James could have got across the room other than walking there? If he had it would be wonderful.

The doctor spoke to Maxine alone once he came downstairs, Holly excusing herself and going to the office, knowing that whatever he had to say should be said privately to Maxine. But that didn't stop her feeling impatient herself, longing to know his findings.

'He's cautiously optimistic.' Maxine sought her out. 'Whatever that means,' she frowned.

'It means that James did walk?'

'It means he tried.' Maxine shook her head, some of the excitement gone now. 'The doctor seemed to think that's as good.'

'It is,' Holly agreed with enthusiasm.

Maxine still looked despondent. 'You don't know James. He can be very stubborn when he wants to, and if he decides this won't go any further then it won't.'

'What does he have to say about it?'

'Well, apparently he's agreed to having a physiotherapist in residence——'

'Apparently?' Holly echoed. 'Haven't you spoken to him yourself yet?'

'I thought I should tell you what was happening first——'

'I'm flattered at your thoughtfulness, Maxine, but I think you should go and see James. Right now.'

'Holly . . .?'

'Hm?'

'You won't leave just yet, will you?' Maxine requested. 'I mean, James isn't going to be working for a few days, so it would be an ideal time for you to leave, I realise that. But I would appreciate it if you didn't.'

'I'll stay a few more days,' Holly nodded. 'At least until I'm sure James is going to be all right.'

She never knew what passed between husband and wife, but she did know that Maxine looked happier than she had ever seen her before, and that James was filled with a new confidence in himself, a determination to walk again, spending hours with the physiotherapist who had been engaged immediately.

'You'll want to call Zack and tell him the good news,'

Holly realised a few days later, knowing that her presence here was no longer needed, that Maxine and James had found a new closeness to bind them together, James making slow but sure progress along the road to full mobility.

Maxine looked uncomfortable now. 'Actually I spoke to him last night.'

'Oh?' Holly instantly stiffened.

'He's coming down here today.'

Holly's cheeks paled. 'What time?'

'Some time this afternoon. Holly——'

'Then would you mind if I left at lunchtime?' she requested abruptly. 'James did agree that I could go, and I have stayed on three extra days.'

'You can leave any time you like, you know we wouldn't force you to stay. It's just——'

'Then I'll leave at lunchtime,' Holly decided firmly.

'But where will you go at such short notice? Holly, you don't have to rush off like this. God, I wish I'd never told you Zack was coming here,' groaned Maxine. 'But I felt I owed it to you.'

'I'm glad you did. I can assure you that Zack won't want to see me any more than I want to see him.'

'He asked about you last night,' Maxine said gently. 'And I think you're wrong about him wanting to see you.'

'Nevertheless, I'd like to leave. I've already been in touch with an agency in London who have promised me some work. I can assure you I'll be all right.' She and the other woman had indeed become good friends the last few days, both of them determined to help James in any way they could.

'But where will you live?'

Holly's mouth twisted. 'There's always accommodation to be found in London.'

'You don't have to leave, Holly, I'm sure Zack doesn't intend to embarass you in any way.'

It was his politeness she wouldn't be able to stand, a cold politeness that would make them into strangers. And she had learnt in the last two weeks that she wanted Zack to be so much more to her than that. If only there weren't the unhappiness of the past that he demanded an explanation of, she might stay and take what time with him that she could.

'I'd rather go,' she said stiltedly. 'James isn't going to be needing a secretary for some time, and the two of you can manage quite well without me.'

'I've enjoyed your company the last few days,' protested Maxine.

'And I've enjoyed yours,' Holly acknowledged softly. 'But I'd still like to leave before Zack arrives.'

'If that's what you want,' Maxine had to reluctantly agree. 'But where will we be able to contact you?'

'I'll call you as soon as I'm settled,' Holly promised.

'But Zack may want to know where you are,' Maxine persisted.

'I doubt it,' she drawled, remembering his disgust with her the last time they met. 'I doubt it very much.'

'But it he does——'

'I'd rather he didn't know,' Holly answered truthfully. 'We've said all we have to say to each other.'

Even James's arguments for her to at least give them an address where she could be reached didn't change her mind. She had learnt from experience, and necessity, that a clean break was the best.

CHAPTER EIGHT

THE large office complex where the agency eventually found her permanent work was exactly what Holly wanted. She had learnt that working and living in someone's home was too wearing on the emotions, that you tended to become caught up in the personal lives of those people. And it wasn't something she ever wanted to happen to her again.

Her new boss was a happily married man in his mid-fifties, and the two of them got along well, neither probing into the other's private life. Charles McGregor was everything she could have wished for in her new boss.

The bed-sit she had acquired for herself was very reminiscent of the bed-sits she had had until she went to work for James, very compact, with the barest essentials in furniture, and most of that on the shabby side. But she made the most of it, just relieved to be away from the emotional complications working for James had involved. And they were still in her life, he and Maxine, something that had never happened with any previous employers.

She telephoned Maxine from time to time to find out how James was progressing, pleased that the therapy seemed to be working, that James was trying very hard to walk again. Maxine sounded like a different person, and Holly felt sure that was partly because, as Maxine had put it, James has got over his awkwardness and the two of them were now sharing a bed again. Maxine had even jokingly made remarks about them possibly having children one day.

Zack was rarely mentioned during these brief telephone conversations, and when he was she usually ended the call abruptly with some made-up excuse. Trying to forget Zack was proving impossible, and talking about him only made the pain worse.

Holly had heard Bobbie's record on the radio several times, and could understand Zack's confidence in her one day being a big star. She was sure of it too; she knew how strong-minded that family could be.

Life had fallen into a routine for her, one of getting up and going to the office, of doing her work quietly and efficiently until five o'clock, and then coming home to spend the evening in front of the television. The thought of possibly doing this for the next thirty or forty years terrified the life out of her. She would lie awake at night reliving every moment she had spent in Zack's arms, longing to see him again, and knowing she never would.

When one of the other girls at the office suggested she go out for the evening with her and a couple of the others she agreed to the change in routine, more to stop herself from going quietly insane than from a real desire to go out. She quite liked the other girls, and got along with them all quite well, but although they were all about her own age she felt older than them.

They went to a noisy club, and though Holly was surrounded by people enjoying themselves she still felt very much alone. After several attempts to dance with different men who asked her she gave that up too, their passes ranging from a barely discernible but definite caress of her back to a blatant desire to try and touch her breast! Everyone seemed in the market for a companion for the evening—and if possible the night too! Everyone except Holly, that was. She wished she had never come here now, knowing that the girls she was with thought she was very unsociable when she refused all further offers to dance. Maybe if they had really had dancing in mind she wouldn't have refused!

But sitting alone at the table, as she often was with the other girls dancing, turned out to be worse, with men actually coming up to her now and offering much more than dancing. She had to be really rude to one man to get him to leave her alone, and her face was flushed with embarrassment when he finally stumbled away.

'That wasn't nice, Holly,' a mocking voice taunted. 'I don't remember you turning men away like that in the past.'

She turned sharply, her face paling now as she instantly recognised Bobbie Chance. 'I'm afraid I didn't find his suggestion in the least "nice" either,' she said stiffly.

Bobbie moved to sit at the table with her, her perfume strong and musky, her black and gold dress so short it was almost indecent, riding up her thighs even more as she sat down. 'Are you living in London now?' she asked curiously.

The last thing Holly had expected, after the scene Bobbie had deliberately caused the last time they met, was for this conversation to be polite! 'For the moment,' she nodded, very wary.

'Zack told me you'd left his brother's house.'

Holly stiffened. 'Did he?'

Bobbie gave her a speculative perusal out of narrowed brown eyes. 'I didn't realise when I met you with him last time that you were working for his brother.'

'I was,' Holly confirmed distantly. 'But not any more.'

'Where are you working now?'

Her wariness grew. 'For a firm in the City,' she answered evasively.

Bobbie nodded. 'Has Zack caught up with you yet?'

Holly gave the other girl a startled look. 'Caught up with me?' she repeated tremulously. 'I didn't even know he was looking for me.' Her hand shook slightly as she raised her glass to her lips. Why on earth could Zack be looking for her? What had she done wrong now?

'For several weeks now,' Bobbie confirmed casually. 'He even asked me if I knew where you were. As if I would know!' she derided in a bored voice.

'As if,' Holly murmured.

'It seems strange seeing you again after all this time, Holly,' Bobbie said thoughtfully. 'How long has it been?'

'Five years,' muttered Holly, wondering where this was leading to.

'Mm,' Bobbie sighed. 'I remember now, I was fifteen at the time.'

Holly swallowed hard. 'Do you—do you ever see Alex? I heard he went to America?'

'He did,' Bobbie said abruptly. 'And no, we never see him.'

'I'm sorry.' Both of them knew how inadequate Holly's apology was, that she was the reason Alex had gone to America.

'Are you?' Bobbie asked bitterly.

'Yes. Bobbie, I never meant it to happen,' she pleaded.

'But it did,' Bobbie snapped. 'The whole family broke up because of it.'

'I'm sorry,' Holly said again, staring down at the table.

'We all were,' Bobbie rasped. 'Sorry we ever met you!' She stood up noisly.

'Bobbie——!' Holly desperately stopped her leaving.

The other girl looked down at her with frostily disdainful eyes. 'Yes?'

Holly moistened her lips. 'If—Zack should ever ask, you haven't seen me?' she prompted.

The brown eyes became mocking. 'Up to your little games again, are you?'

'No——'

'Just why is Zack looking for you, then? You haven't run off with a family heirloom, have you?' taunted Bobbie.

Holly flushed. 'Don't be silly!'

'I'm not so sure it is,' Bobbie shrugged. 'Zack seemed pretty grim when he spoke to me.'

Holly swallowed hard. 'I haven't done anything wrong where Zack is concerned, I just don't want to see him again. Please, Bobbie,' she looked at her pleadingly.

'Why should I want to mess up his life by telling him I've seen you?' Bobbie dismissed. 'I like Zack, he certainly doesn't deserve you in his life!'

Holly flinched at the insult. 'Thank you,' she said quietly.

'Don't thank me,' snapped Bobbie. 'I'm not doing you any favours.'

Inadvertently she was, although Holly didn't tell her that. Bobbie was likely to tell Zack she had seen her out of spite if she knew how much Holly desperately wanted her not to. 'Goodbye, Bobbie,' she said softly. 'And congratulations on the success of your record.' She had watched as it progressed steadily up the charts the last few weeks.

'Thanks,' Bobbie drawled uninterestedly.

Holly moistened her lips. 'Do you ever—Do you see——'

'Mother?' Bobbie finished derisively. 'Fairly often,' she nodded. 'She never mentions you now.'

'I see,' Holly answered tremulously.

'Goodbye, Holly,' Bobbie said hardly. 'I hope our bumping into each other like this doesn't become a habit.'

'I hope so too,' nodded Holly, shaking badly now, relieved when Bobbie actually returned to her friends across the room, Holly forgotten by her in seconds.

'Was that Bobbie Chance I saw you talking to just now?' An awestruck Chloe returned to their table.

Holly's heart sank; the last thing she wanted was to be questioned about knowing Bobbie. 'Bobbie Chance?' she pretended ignorance. 'I didn't realise.'

'But I saw you talking together,' Chloe frowned.

'We were,' she nodded. 'She just stopped by our table to take a breather from dancing.'

Chloe didn't look convinced by this explanation. 'How odd,' she said slowly.

No odder than the truth was! Holly made a point of avoiding such evenings after that, always having a good excuse when any of the girls at the office suggested she join them again. In the end they stopped asking, convinced she had a lover she didn't want to talk about.

'No wonder you haven't wanted to come out with us lately!' Chloe gave her a sharp dig in the ribs as they streamed from the office building three weeks later.

'Hm?' Holly frowned her puzzlement; she had been busy contemplating the loneliness of the weekend that lay ahead of her, sure she must have missed part of this conversation with Chloe; it certainly didn't make any sense to her!

'I would have kept quiet about him too,' her new friend added enigmatically.

'Sorry?' Holly looked more puzzled than ever.

'It's all right, Holly,' grinned Chloe. 'Your secret is safe with me.'

The colour left her cheeks. 'What secret?'

'Him,' Chloe nodded to the left of where they were standing.

Holly followed her gaze, her face suddenly stricken. 'Zack . . .!' she gasped softly; she would have thought she was hallucinating if Chloe hadn't seen him too.

He looked a little like a ghost, very pale and grim, lines about his eyes, his mouth a thinned line, his body slightly leaner too in the fitted denims and green sweatshirt.

'Have a good weekend,' Chloe told her conspiratorially. 'He's gorgeous, Holly!' came her parting shot.

He was indeed gorgeous, and Holly's heart had done a somersault the moment she saw him again. And there could be no doubt he was waiting for her, his narroweyed gaze fixed on her compellingly. They stood looking at each other as the rest of the office staff pushed past them on their way home, neither of them seeming inclined to speak.

'Er—this is a surprise,' Holly finally spoke, inadequately.

'Is it?' he rasped. 'Didn't Bobbie tell you I was looking for you?'

'Bobbie?' she swallowed.

'You saw her at a club several weeks ago, didn't you?' he drawled hardly.

'Yes. But——'

'We can't discuss this here, Holly,' he scowled darkly, grasping her arm to push her down the street towards the car park, unlocking her car door for her and standing over her as she got inside.

'I didn't intend running,' Holly snapped impatiently.

'You wouldn't have got very far if you did,' he told her grimly, striding round the car to get in beside her. 'Your running days are over. It's taken me almost three months to track you down, I wouldn't let you get away from me now.'

It sounded almost like a threat, and Holly shivered involuntarily. 'I had no idea you were even looking for me.' She sat rigidly at his side as he reversed the car out of its parking space and then accelerated it out on to the road.

'Bobbie told you,' he contradicted flatly.

'I meant up until then,' she blushed.

He gave her a sideways glance of censure. 'And that was three weeks ago.'

'She said she wouldn't tell you she'd seen me,' Holly choked at the betrayal.

'Bobbie tends to say things she doesn't mean when she loses her temper,' Zack derided harshly. 'We've been recording her new record the last week or so, and I haven't been happy with the way it's been going. Bobbie lost her temper after I critisised her one afternoon, and told me she'd seen you.'

Holly could tell by the grimness of his expression that he hadn't welcomed the delay in being given the information. 'But she didn't know where I worked,' she frowned. 'I didn't tell her.'

'She knew it was for a company. I couldn't even begin looking for you here without knowing that, you might have been working for some little corner shop that I would never find!'

'I don't understand why you were looking for me.'

'Don't you?' he scorned.

'No,' she shook her head.

'We have unfinished business,' he told her curtly.

Holly frowned. 'I don't understand.'

His mouth was a taut line. 'You left James's house without telling anyone where you were going, least of all me.'

'I didn't think you would be interested,' she answered truthfully.

'Not interested?' he rasped. 'You knew damn well I'd be interested, why else would you leave so suddenly on the day I was due to arrive?'

'It wasn't sudden,' she defended. 'I'd already told James I was leaving days earlier.'

'And yet you waited until you knew I was coming to see you before going,' he snapped.

'You weren't coming to see me——'

His eyes flashed darkly green. 'I was, damn you!'

Her breath seemed to leave her body. 'I—But Maxine called you about James——'

'*I* telephoned *her*—about you,' he corrected harshly.

'But I thought—I didn't realise . . . '

'You didn't stay around long enough to find out, did you?' Zack accused coldly. 'I'd talked to James several days earlier about the good news of his probably being able to walk again, I spoke to Maxine the night before you left to tell her I was coming to see you. She was supposed to make sure you were there when I arrived,' he added grimly, his tone boding ill for the other woman.

'She tried,' Holly realised dully.

'Not hard enough,' he bit out, and Holly could only wonder further at the displeasure he had shown Maxine for her failure to keep her at the house. 'Do you know the hell you've put me through since you left like that?' he demanded angrily.

'No.' She only knew the way she had suffered, the way she missed seeing him every waking moment, the way she dreamed of his elusiveness every night.

'It's been sheer bloody torture!' he ground out, his face set as if carved from granite.

Holly swallowed hard, moistening her lips, her hands clenched together to stop them trembling. 'What unfinished business do we have?' she asked huskily.

'Us.'

'Us?' she echoed dazedly.

Zack nodded. 'You think after we'd *made love* so completely I was going to just pretend it never happened?'

She flushed at the way he insisted on calling it making love when she had told him it was only sex. 'You succeeded in doing exactly that for almost two weeks,' she reminded him stiffly.

'I succeeded in nothing except a lot of soul-searching that got me absolutely nowhere,' he dismissed curtly. 'I've tried to puzzle you out, Holly, but I can't do it. It makes no difference to how I feel about you anyway,' he added self-derisively.

'Feel about me?' she echoed nervously.

'There's no need to look as if I'm about to beat you,' he said impatiently. 'What I feel for you is perfectly natural, I can assure you. Although I don't intend discussing it any further in a car,' he muttered as he drove into an underground car park.

Holly recognised it as the car park beneath the building that contained his apartment, and her nervousness grew. She was frightened of being alone with him again, frightened of her emotions where Zack was concerned.

'Holly?' He stood beside the open car door, his hand held out invitingly.

She ignored his hand, climbing out without his assistance, avoiding his probing gaze as she did so. She couldn't let him touch her, not even out of politeness.

'Miss Independent,' he mocked as they walked over to the lift.

Holly ignored the jibe, just as she ignored any attempt at conversation as they went up in the lift, its only occupants, steeling herself for the scene in front of them. Zack must be made to realise that she couldn't continue her affair with him, that for her own already bruised self-respect it couldn't go on.

'Drink?' he offered once they were in the lounge of his apartment, his own expression no less grim.

'It's a little early for me, but you go ahead,' she invited stiltedly, standing awkwardly just inside the doorway.

'It's too early for me too.' His mouth twisted. 'Would you prefer a tea or coffee?'

'Er——' She just wanted to get this over with and then leave; she would prefer it if he wouldn't be quite so polite. 'No, I don't think so.'

'Suits me,' he shrugged. 'I'd rather we talked this out as soon as possible too. After weeks of looking for you, and finally finding you, I want to spend as little time talking as possible.'

Holly swallowed hard. 'You do?'

'Let's not play games any more,' he gave an impatient sigh. 'You know what I want to do.'

Her eyes were wide. 'No, I——'

'Holly, I've wanted you so badly these last weeks it's been eating me up alive!' groaned Zack.

'Want!' she echoed with scorn.

His eyes darkened. 'There's more to it than that, Holly, and you know it.'

'I know that I've been very stupid where you're concerned,' she said tautly. 'I let you too close, Zack, and now you want more.'

'I *demand* more,' he corrected forcefully. 'You gave me more than just your body, Holly.'

She paled. 'No——'

'Yes,' he ground out. 'There've been a lot of other women for me, Holly, and I *know* it wasn't just sex between us, as you claim it was. You keep pushing me away all the time, and I want to know why.'

She turned away. 'You know why.'

'Because you once had an affair with a married man?' he said dismissively. 'You're far from the first woman to do that, Holly.'

'It mattered to you three months ago!'

'For a time he did,' he sighed at his own stupidity in letting it be so. 'It just didn't fit in with that I wanted to believe of you. But you certainly don't make a habit of stealing other woman's husbands. James told me that he asked you to marry him and that you turned him down,' he added gently.

Colour darkened her cheeks. 'I wish he hadn't done that.'

'Why?'

'It was something private.' She avoided his gaze. 'And he didn't mean it anyway.'

'No, I realise that,' nodded Zack. 'But I do.'

She raised startled eyes to his. 'You do what?'

'I mean it,' he held her gaze as he came to stand in front of her. 'Holly, I want to marry you.'

'No——'

'I love you, Holly.' He came down on the carpet in front of her, taking her shaking hands into his. 'I love you so much,' he groaned, deep lines grooved beside his nose and mouth. 'I need you even more.'

Holly felt as if all the air had been knocked from her body with a wounding blow. 'It's impossible,' she protested. 'I can't——'

'Shush!' He put silencing fingertips over her lips. 'Don't say no yet.'

'I have to——'

'The only thing you have to do is come here,' he soothed as he pulled her down into his arms, kissing her slowly, languorously, encouraging her response. 'I missed you, Holly,' he moaned as he lowered her to the carpeted floor beneath him. 'I've missed you like hell,' he repeated savagely, his mouth more fierce on hers now.

Holly had missed him too, more than she had even known; her arms wound about his neck as he gathered her into his body, the hardness of his thighs imprinted on hers.

'I've had fantasies about you these last weeks,' he told her gruffly as his mouth travelled the length of her throat before exploring the sensuous shell of her ear. 'And in all of them we were in bed together!'

She had known that without being told; she had had the same fantasies, although none of them had ever included him proposing to her! That was something she had never expected. It was also completely impossible.

'I can't do this, Zack.' She tried to push him away, all to no avail.

'Of course you can.' His arms remained like vices about her, his breath warm against her cheek. 'We're already halfway there, Holly. Admittedly this carpet isn't a bed, but at least you're in my arms. They've been so empty without you, Holly.'

'I can't believe——'

'Don't even suggest another woman,' he rasped, his eyes hard. 'Since you first looked at me so incredulously because you thought I was James walking I haven't looked at, or wanted, another woman! I knew I'd actually fallen in love with you that night in my bedroom when you responded to me. Until that moment it had never occurred to me that I could be in love with you. I was dazed by it.'

Holly remembered the occasion well; she also remembered that she had put his disbelief down to the fact that he hadn't known she was capable of warmer feelings. 'I had no idea,' she said weakly.

Zack shrugged, still holding her firmly against his chest. 'There was no reason why you should; up to that point we'd been antagonists. But after that I was more than ever determined you would go out with me, although that didn't stop me being jealous of the affection you had for James.'

'I'm afraid you were right about that.' She moistened her lips, unable to look at him. 'The fact that he was in a wheelchair did set him apart from other men as far as I was concerned.'

'What do you mean?' he frowned.

She drew in a deeply ragged breath. 'He wasn't a threat to me,' she admitted huskily, the warmth of love he was showing her loosening her tongue as nothing else could have done. She could still hardly believe he loved her, although it shone bright and clear for her in the luminous green eyes.

'A threat?' echoed Zack in a puzzled voice. 'I don't understand why any man should be a threat to you.'

'It doesn't matter,' she dismissed lightly, deeply regretting the lapse. 'Now what was it you said about going to bed?' she asked teasingly.

'Holly——'

'Don't tell me you've changed your mind?' she mocked, knowing he hadn't, with the evidence of his desire still throbbing against her.

'You know I haven't. But——'

'Don't let's talk any more, Zack,' she encouraged softly. 'It never works out when we talk.' And she wanted him so badly too now.

'We have to talk, Holly.'

'But not now,' she begged, entwining her arms about his body, her nails digging pleasurably into his back.

'God, Holly, I can't think when you do that . . .' The warm moistness of his lips moved fiercely over hers, taking, devouring, possessing, until both of them trembled with desire, a desire Zack controlled. 'Marry me, Holly,' he encouraged against her breasts. 'Marry me and you'll never regret it.'

'You might,' she choked.

He raised his head to look down at her, his face flushed with passion. 'What do you mean?'

She sighed. 'You know nothing about me.'

'I know I love you, that's enough.'

'It isn't,' she shook her head. 'Tell me all the things you really know about me, Zack,' she encouraged.

'You're kind, loyal, loving, warm——'

'And a marriage-wrecker,' she put in softly.

A look of irritation crossed his face. 'I don't believe that.'

'I've told you it's the truth,' she reminded him quietly.

Zack moved awkwardly to his feet, lacking the lithe grace of movement he usually possessed in his agitation. 'You didn't mean to do it.'

'That doesn't change the fact that it happened.' Holly brushed down her skirt as she moved to sit in the chair. 'I can't marry anyone with that in my past. You saw how bitter Bobbie still is, and she was far from the only one I hurt.'

'We all hurt people, it's an occupational hazard.'

'Not the way I hurt them,' she shook her head.

'It wasn't deliberate,' he continued to defend her.

'You don't have a malicious streak in your body, I would swear to that.'

'Try convincing my mother of that,' she said bitterly.

'Your mother . . .?'

'Just another casualty in the whole sordid affair,' she dismissed with scorn. 'You see, Zack, you have no idea of the repercussions of what I did.'

'Your mother found out about it?' he probed tentatively.

'Oh yes,' she derided brittlely.

'She blamed you?'

'*Everyone* blamed me!' Her voice was so sharp with tension now it sounded as if it might break—and her along with it. It was so long since she had talked to anyone about this, all her pleas for understanding in the past falling on deaf ears, although Zack wasn't judging at the moment, only listening intently.

'I suppose your mother had a right to feel disappointed——'

'She wasn't disappointed,' Holly scorned harshly. 'She was heartbroken! Do you think I might have that drink now?' she rasped shakily.

'Of course.' Zack moved to pour her a large measure of brandy, staying very close to her after he had handed her the glass.

Holly swallowed some of the brandy straight down, grateful for the slap on the back that helped stop her choking, not raising a word of protest when Zack took the glass out of her trembling fingers and put it on the coffee-table out of the way.

'Your mother was naturally upset,' Zack tried to reason with her. 'I would be more than a little upset if our daughter became involved with a married man at that age.'

Tears filled her eyes. *Their* daughter. It had such a

beautiful sound to it. 'I can't marry you, Zack,' she shook her head, pleading with him to leave the subject alone.

'You're going to,' he told her determinedly. 'I have no intention of letting you ruin our lives because of something that happened over five years ago.'

'You don't even know *what* happened,' she choked. 'I don't deserve to be happy.'

'The fact that you've admitted you could be with me only makes me all the more determined that we shall be,' he said grimly. 'You say I don't know what happened, and maybe I don't. You're going to tell me it all now, and then we'll forget about it.'

Maybe that would be best, maybe once he knew it all he would leave her alone. He certainly wouldn't want to forget it; she had been trying to do so for years and never succeeded.

'All right, Zack,' she decided, standing up and moving as far away from him as she could. 'I'll tell you.' She raised her head, meeting his gaze unflinchingly, although the violet eyes showed her inner pain. 'First of all I think you should know that Bobbie Chance was my stepsister.'

'Your *what?*'

Holly blushed at his astonishment. 'She was the stepsister I told you I acquired for two years. Her father, Giles, was married to my mother.'

Zack seemed to pale, a pulse beating erratically at his jaw. 'You were involved with your *stepfather?*' he demanded incredulously.

'No,' she said dully.

'But you said—Bobbie said——'

'All either of us ever told you was that I'd broken up her father's marriage; you jumped to the conclusion there was an affair between Giles and me,' she reminded him tautly.

Zack was breathing heavily, having difficulty taking in this change of facts. 'So what happened? Didn't you like the man, did you make your mother choose between the two of you?' He was frowning darkly in his confusion. 'What the hell *happened?*' His voice rose sharply.

'I certainly didn't make my mother choose between us,' Holly snapped. 'Although perhaps in the end she felt compelled to. After all, she was my mother,' she added bitterly. 'Although I'm sure it's a decision she's bitterly regretted.'

Zack looked totally confused now. 'If your step-father's name was Giles who the hell is Alex?'

Holly bit painfully into her bottom lip. 'He was—is, Bobbie's older brother, the stepbrother I also acquired for two years.'

Zack's eyes narrowed. 'And he's the one you felt sexual curiosity about?'

'Yes.'

'But that isn't unnatural,' he assured her. 'All young girls feel like that at that age.'

Her eyes flashed as she glared at him. 'Not all young girls encourage the man so much that he rapes her!'

CHAPTER NINE

THE astounded silence that followed her impassioned outburst was deafening in its stillness, only the sound of Holly's ragged breathing as she fought back the tears showing the deep state of her agitation.

'Your—stepbrother—raped—you?' Zack finally said disbelievingly, his expression grim.

'Yes,' she choked, turning away. 'Oh, it was my own fault——'

'No man can be excused for forcing a woman into sexual submission,' he rasped.

'You don't understand, Zack——'

'I don't need to,' he shook his head. 'Any man who resorts to force is not a man at all!'

Holly moistened her lips. 'But I encouraged him, wanted him to kiss and touch me, until I realised he intended making love to me.'

'How old was he?'

She looked startled. 'I don't see——'

'How old?' Zack repeated harshly.

'Twenty-four——'

'Then he should have been able to control himself once he could see you weren't willing,' he ground out. 'At twenty-four he was a man, you were still a child—a curious child.'

'With a woman's body and curiosity,' she said dully. 'He was away at college when my mother first married his father, and as I was away at school too, we didn't see much of each other, just part of the holidays really if he should come home, which he didn't always do. He always seemed so dark and handsome to me, I suppose I was infatuated with him.'

'Go on,' Zack encouraged softly.

She swallowed hard. 'I think he knew how attractive I'd always found him——'

'I'm sure he did!'

Holly blushed. 'Thinking back, I must have been pretty obvious.'

'At that age most girls are,' Zack excused.

'Maybe,' she acknowledged softly. 'I was looking forward to the summer Alex left college; he'd promised he would spend the whole of the summer at home with us. I was never very close to Bobbie, but Alex always seemed to like having me around.'

'I'm sure he did,' Zack ground out. 'It fed his damned ego.'

'Probably,' she sighed, looking down at her hands. 'He took me almost everywhere with him those summer weeks, introduced me to several of his friends, even seemed jealous when a couple of them showed an interest in me.'

'He didn't want to lose his loving little slave to anyone else,' rasped Zack.

Holly flushed. 'Perhaps not,' she agreed softly. 'It must have been obvious to him that I worshipped him.'

'I'm sure it was,' he nodded grimly, as if the idea greatly displeased him.

'Then one night we went to a party together. Alex had been drinking rather a lot, but then so had most of the others,' she couldn't control the shudder that went through her at the memory of that night. 'He seemed all right as we drove home, not drunk or anything, so I began to relax a little. Then when we got into the house he began to kiss me. I didn't mind, he'd often kissed me in in the past, and our parents and Bobbie were upstairs, so I knew he wouldn't go too far.' She choked back a sob. 'At first he just kissed me, and then he began to—to touch me. I—I wanted to say no, but I was frightened of angering him, of him thinking me a baby. And after a while it didn't feel so bad anyway, in fact it was quite pleasant,' she admitted with guilt.

'That sort of sexual curiosity is just part of growing up,' Zack told her softly.

'What do you mean, "that" sort?' she frowned.

'We'll talk in a minute, darling,' he assured her. 'Just tell me the rest of what happened.'

Holly gave a ragged sigh. 'When I realised he wasn't going to stop at kissing and caressing me I began to panic, pleaded with him to stop, fought him when he wouldn't. I scratched his cheek so badly the blood streamed down his face,' she recalled with a shudder.

'He deserved worse!' rasped Zack.

'I'm not sure any of us ever get what we deserve,' she said dully. 'He didn't seem like my beloved Alex as he ripped my clothes off, he was suddenly a stranger to me, a stranger with glitteringly intent eyes. I wanted to die as he took me, wished I *could* die at that moment.'

'The bastard!' Zack bit out harshly.

She shook her head. 'It was my own fault,' she told him again. 'He'd kissed me before, but he'd always stopped at kisses in the past. If I'd had any sense I would have tried to tease him out of that mood, would have stopped him somehow. But I couldn't even scream,' she breathed heavily, reliving the nightmare. 'He had his hand over my mouth!'

Zack's hands clenched and unclenched at his sides as he fought for control. 'And afterwards?'

'He pleaded with me not to tell anyone——'

'Meaning your parents,' Zack derided harshly.

'Yes,' she confirmed shakily. 'I promised I wouldn't.

I just wanted to get away from him, to be alone. Most of my clothes were unwearable, but I pulled on my blouse even though the buttons were all ripped off. I couldn't bear to have him looking at my nakedness a moment longer! I suddenly hated him as I'd never hated anyone before, found myself looking at someone I didn't even know. But before I could escape to my room the lounge door opened and my stepfather stood there.' She could still remember the shame she had felt as Giles' narrow-eyed gaze took in the scene before him.

'And completely misunderstood the situation, I'm sure,' Zack prompted as she fell silent.

'I don't know what he thought,' she shrugged. 'Before he could say anything Alex began to talk, and everything he said was lies,' she remembered dazedly. 'He said I was always encouraging him, asking him to make love to me, that I was a wanton, that he finally couldn't hold out against me any longer.' Her voice shook as she recalled Alex's further betrayal. 'He—he said he wasn't the first either,' she added chokingly, her eyes closed to shut out the pain.

'Did your stepfather believe him?'

'What else could he do?' She shook her head. 'But it wasn't true, any of it. If you knew the pain I suffered when Alex took me——'

'I know, Holly,' Zack soothed. 'It's all right, darling.'

'All right?' Her eyes blazed as she looked up at him. 'Alex told everyone I was no better than a whore and you say it's all right! I was so hurt I couldn't even defend myself, and by the time my mother came down to see what was keeping my stepfather it had been decided it was all my fault.'

'What did your mother say?'

Holly shrugged. 'She was stunned.'

'What else?'

She trembled slightly. 'She believed them. She didn't even ask me what had happened, she just believed them.' Her voice broke emotionally.

'But you said they divorced because of you?'

'They did,' she nodded. 'When I finally came out of my shock I told them what had really happened. I'm sure my mother didn't really believe me, but I was her daughter, and she felt compelled to take my side. My stepfather refused to believe me, and in the end it drove them apart. I wasn't around to know all the details, I was back at school by then.'

'Learning self-defence,' Zack realised lightly.

Her mouth tightened. 'I wasn't going to let any man force himself on me again!'

'And I didn't,' he reminded her gently.

'Meeting you, my reaction to you, finally confirmed that all Alex had accused me of was true. I must have encouraged him to think I'd let him make love to me without realising it, because I know that I took one look at you and I wanted you.'

'That doesn't mean you're a wanton——'

'It does!'

'No,' Zack contradicted softly. 'I took one look at you and wanted you too.'

'It's different for a man.'

'No, it isn't. We might be a bit more verbal about our wants and desires, but that doesn't mean a woman doesn't feel them too. Holly, the curiosity you had then to know what it felt like if a man touched you is a natural part of growing up. I used to have the most erotic fantasies about my English teacher when I was at school! I would probably have run a mile if she'd so much as touched me. You just chose the wrong man to have adolescent fantasies about,' she comforted her gently. 'What *we* had together was something totally different.'

'How?' Holly asked dully.

'For one thing we're both adults. For another, I believe we love each other.' He looked at her challengingly.

'I told you, I don't——'

'Holly,' he interrupted softly. 'We love each other,' he repeated determinedly.

She gazed at his ruggedly handsome face and knew that she did love him, that she had for some time. But there was no future for them together. 'I'm not a lovable person,' she told him flatly. 'Even my own mother disowned me.'

'Tell me,' he encouraged.

She had told him so much, why not the rest? 'She sent me back to school as soon as I was over the worst of the shock. I haven't seen her since.'

'Not for five years?' Zack was astounded.

Holly nodded. 'Oh, she wrote a little, at first, stilted letters that told me she and Giles were divorcing. After a time even those letters stopped coming. That last year of school wasn't a pleasant one for me; Bobbie didn't know the full story, only that our parents were divorcing and that it had something to do with me, and she showed her resentment in a hundred different ways. I was glad when the time came for me to leave. I already had a job, so I went straight to it.'

'Your mother didn't come to see you even when you left school?'

'She was coming to see Bobbie,' she told him without emotion. 'The two of them had remained close in spite of the divorce, and Bobbie took great delight in telling me *my* mother was coming to take *her* home from school. I didn't see her, as I hadn't seen her during any of the holidays, always spending them with friends or staying on at the school.'

'I can't believe any mother would be so inhuman,' Zack frowned.

'I caused the break-up of her marriage, Zack,' Holly reminded him mockingly.

'You were still her daughter!'

'A daughter who'd supposedly enticed her stepbrother to make love to her and then cried rape.'

'You *were* raped!'

'My mother couldn't be sure of that.'

'Whether she was sure or not she should have stood by you,' he scowled.

'Would you have done?' asked Holly.

'I would have stood by my child no matter what she'd done.'

Holly knew that he would too, that once his love was given it was for life. And he didn't seem to hate her for what she'd done either. 'That's what Giles did, he stood by his son.'

'At the cost of his marriage. He couldn't have truly loved your mother.'

'Oh, I'm sure he did.'

'Then they would have worked something out and stayed together. Their divorce served no purpose, because you haven't seen any of them since then anyway.'

Holly shook her head. 'You're confusing me again, Zack.'

'I want to do so much more than that.' At last Zack took her in his arms, holding her firmly against his strong chest. 'I want to take care of you for the rest of your life, I want to make sure that nothing and no one every hurts you again. I love you, Holly.'

'I love you too!' she choked, having difficulty saying

the words that had been locked up inside her for ever, it seemed. 'I do love you, Zack,' her eyes swam with tears. 'But what if I'm everything Alex said I was, what if I am a wanton and a whore?'

'How many men have you wanted in your life, Holly?' he asked patiently.

'Alex, and——'

'Did you really want him?'

'No . . .'

'Then he doesn't count. So how many other men have you wanted?' He arched darkly blond brows.

She looked up at him with wide eyes. 'You. Just you.'

He smiled triumphantly. 'That's what I thought.'

'But that doesn't prove anything,' Holly pointed out earnestly. 'I've never allowed any other men near me.'

'How about James?'

She opened her mouth to speak and then closed it again, remembering the one occasion James had kissed her, and she had felt nothing for him but warm friendship. 'Did Alex lie?' she realised slowly.

'Of course he lied,' Zack said grimly. 'He would have said anything at the time to save his own skin. But you shouldn't have listened to him, darling.'

'I was so young, I didn't know——'

'You were the victim, Holly, not the perpetrator.' He framed her face with his strong hands. 'Now it's time you started to enjoy your life. I hope marrying me will help you do that?'

He sounded so uncertain, so vulnerable. 'I'd love to marry you, Zack,' she told him eagerly now that the barriers had been removed, from her own mind as well as between them. 'I love you so much that these last three months have been hell for me too.'

He gave a ragged sigh. 'I thought you'd never say it,' he admitted shakily.

'That I love you?'

'That too, but I really meant you would marry me. We'll be so happy together, Holly,' he promised in between butterfly kisses. 'I promise you.'

She didn't need any promises from him, knew instinctively that although he had the power to hurt her he never would. 'It doesn't have to be marriage, Zack. I'll live with you——'

'You're going to do that too, until I can get you safely married to me, which I hope won't take too long,' he told her determinedly. 'I'm not letting you out of my sight until then. You might get some more strange notions in your head and run off again.'

'I won't.'

'I'm not giving you the opportunity, young lady,' he said firmly. 'Now, much as I would love to carry you off to bed, I think we should go and get your things and move you in here as soon as possible.'

'Couldn't we do that later—move me in, I mean?'

Zack's eyes darkened. 'We could . . .'

'Then let's do that,' she smiled up at him shyly. 'I shall die from the need to touch you in a moment.'

He drew in a shuddering breath. 'Suddenly I don't care if you never bring the rest of your clothes here, I don't care if you never get dressed again!'

Holly gave a husky laugh as he carried her off to bed, love shining brightly in her eyes.

She woke to find a warm body curled into the back of hers, a possessive hand on her breast. Her mouth instantly curved into a smile, remembering the night that had just passed, when Zack had claimed her as his again and again, until finally they both fell into an exhausted sleep.

'I hope that smile is for me,' he murmured languorously against her ear.

'It is.' She turned sleepily in his arms. 'I've never felt so loved and alive.'

A shadow darkened his eyes. 'That's because you never have been.' He showed his resentment for her suffering of the last five years.

'It doesn't matter now, Zack.' She smoothed the frown from his brow. 'You're like the pot of gold at the end of the rainbow.'

He grinned. 'That's the first time I've been called that—plenty of other things, but never that!'

'You're also wonderful, considerate, sensitive——'

'You can add conceited to that list if you say any more,' he told her dryly. 'And we have something much more pleasurable we can do than talk.'

'But I thought you liked to talk,' teased Holly.

'The time for that is over, woman,' he growled. 'It's time for action now.'

'After last night?' She pretended to be shocked by his renewed desire. 'Shouldn't you be slowing down a little at your age?'

He rolled over to pin her beneath him. 'I'll let you know when I'm slowing down. Maybe in forty or fifty years' time,' he added wolfishly.

Holly gave a laugh of pure enjoyment, knowing she had never been so happy, giving herself up to the fiery warmth of Zack's lovemaking. The ring of the telephone on the bedside table interrupted them before they could do any more than kiss each other.

'Damn,' Zack muttered as it kept ringing and ringing. 'Whoever it is has no sense of timing. I'll have to answer it.' He looked down regretfully at her slender nakedness.

She touched his cheek lovingly. 'I'll still be here when you've finished your call.'

He gave her another regretful look before picking up the receiver. 'Yes?' he barked into the mouthpiece. 'Oh, it's you,' he said in a disgruntled voice, lying on his back to pull Holly down on to his chest. 'No, I wasn't sleeping,' he still spoke to his caller. 'Mind your own damn business!' he rasped as he was obviously asked what he had been doing. 'There's nothing wrong with my temper, I just think you could have chosen a better time to call me.' His arm tightened warmly about Holly's shoulders. 'Yes, I did manage to find Holly,' he said with satisfaction.

She sat up to look at him anxiously. Who had known he had been looking for her?

'Yes, Maxine,' he answered Holly's unasked question, grinning as she gave a relaxed smile. 'No, not today,' he told the other woman decisively. 'Maybe tomorrow. I'll ask Holly.' He put his hand over the mouthpiece. 'Maxine's invited us to lunch tomorrow, do you want to go?'

'If you do,' she nodded. 'I'd love to see them again.'

'Yes, okay, Maxine,' he spoke to his sister-in-law once again. 'No, you can't speak to Holly, she's busy.'

'Oh, but——'

'Yes, we'll both see you tomorrow,' Zack cut across Holly's protest. 'I'll tell her.' He was smiling as he replaced the receiver.

'Tell me what?' Holly snuggled down against him.

'Maxine said congratulations.'

She gave him a sharp look. 'How did she know——'

'Darling,' he chuckled, 'if you could have seen the way I've been frantically searching for you then you wouldn't doubt that I love you either.'

'I don't,' she told him confidently. 'Why didn't you want to see Maxine and James today?' She toyed with the wiry hair on his chest.

'Because I have plans for today, and none of them include getting out of this bed!'

'Oh.'

Zack laughed softly at her blushes. 'I may let you out for a few minutes, just to cook us lunch.'

Her eyes widened. 'Why can't we do that together?'

'I'd rather you did it.'

'That's sexist!'

'That's necessary,' he chided. 'Besides the fact that I can't boil an egg, I have a feeling I may be too exhausted by then to crawl from the bed.'

Her frown instantly turned into a laugh. 'So I am wearing you out, after all!'

'Let's put it this way,' he said dryly. 'I think the studio may have to get along without me most of the time after we're married!'

It was quite late when they began to drive down to Hampshire the next day; despite their teasing they had once again spent most of the night making love, waking late the next morning, neither of them in a hurry to leave each other's arms even then.

Holly turned in her seat to look at the man she loved, never having seen him so completely relaxed. 'How are James and Maxine now?' she asked. 'I've spoken to her several times on the telephone, and she always sounds very happy . . .'

'She is,' Zack nodded.

'You mean she's over her infatuation for you?' she teased.

He gave her an indulgent smile. 'Completely. She and James have never been so close. He's walking with sticks now, by the way.'

'Maxine told me that last time I called,' she nodded. 'It's marvellous!'

The change in the other couple was unbelievable. They touched and kissed every opportunity they got, always smiling at each other, seeming like two different people to the ones Holly had known three months ago.

'I was beginning to feel as if we were the old married couple,' Zack mocked on the drive back to London.

Holly smiled with him. 'It was nice of Maxine to offer to help with the wedding arrangements, wasn't it?'

'As long as she gets her head out of cloud nine long enough to realise it's going to be this Saturday, not next year!' he said dryly.

'Oh, she does,' Holly nodded. 'She's coming up to town on Tuesday to help me look for a dress.'

He gave her a sideways glance. 'You didn't mind my telling them it would be this Saturday? After all, we hadn't discussed a definite date . . .'

'Saturday will be lovely,' she assured him. 'The sooner you're married to me the better—I don't want to run the risk of you falling for one of your songbirds!'

'There'll never be anyone else for me now, Holly,' he took her remark seriously. 'I'll admit there have been a lot of women in my past, but that's where they'll stay, in my past.'

'I know that.' She put her hand on his thigh. 'I know you love me, Zack. I'm not that insecure that I can't take love when it's given.'

'It just hasn't been given very often,' he said grimly.

'I told you, that doesn't matter now I have you. None of it matters.' And she meant it. The unhappiness of the last five years no longer existed now that she had Zack.

It was a hectic week, one of the busiest Holly had ever known. There was so much to do to arrange a wedding, and they had so little time to do it in. Maxine was a tremendous help, she and James coming up to

London on the Tuesday to help and stay on for the wedding.

Zack had insisted that Holly had to leave her job, and as she wasn't really career-minded and wanted to spend as much time with him as she possibly could she had done so without a qualm, spending her days organising the wedding, her evenings and nights with Zack, having moved in with him completely now, the last in a long line of bed-sitters given up for good.

Zack and James left early for the register office on Saturday morning, leaving Maxine to help Holly dress and then drive her to the wedding.

'You look beautiful, Holly,' Maxine told her warmly, tears in her eyes.

She did look quite attractive, the ivory-coloured dress and hat suiting her colouring perfectly, her hair a soft red cloud about her flushed cheeks having grown longer during the last three months. She looked young and beautiful, and she could hardly wait to become Zack's wife.

In every sense of the word except the legal one they were already married, spending every waking moment together that they could, every sleeping one too, sharing thoughts and dreams, their love a tangible thing between them now. For Holly there was only happiness in the security of Zack's love, and she welcomed their future together with open arms.

The two men were waiting outside the register office for them, looking more like twins than just brothers, both tall and straight, their golden hair gleaming brightly, their grey morning suits very formal, when she was used to seeing Zack in nothing but denims and casual shirts all week.

'Can I have a word alone with Holly?' Zack held her gaze steadily as he spoke to the other couple.

'Can't it wait until after the ceremony?' teased Maxine. 'You have her alone for a whole month then.'

'No, it can't wait,' he said intently.

'Let's wait for them inside, Maxine,' James suggested firmly.

Holly felt a moment of panic. Surely Zack hadn't waited until now to tell her he had changed his mind, that he couldn't go through with it?

'No, I'll never do that,' he seemed to read her mind. 'I just wanted to tell you how much I love you.'

Relief flooded through her. 'Did you have to be so melodramatic about it?' she chided. 'You frightened me for a minute!'

'I didn't mean to.' He took her into his arms. 'But I get afraid too sometimes. I rushed you into this wedding so fast you haven't had time to think. I want you to be sure this is what you want.'

'I am.'

'*Very* sure.'

'I'm very sure.' She looked up at him frowningly. 'Zack, I love you. I *want* to marry you. Besides,' she added softly, 'there may not just be the two of us to consider any more.'

'Hm?' He looked puzzled.

'Zack, we've just spent a beautiful pre-wedding week together,' she explained patiently. 'I have a feeling we might have done a little more than that.'

'A baby?' The gleam of satisfaction in his eyes dispelled any doubts she might have had that he wouldn't want a baby so soon, although they had discussed the possibility of having children at some time in their marriage. 'Do you think it's possible?'

'Don't you?' she teased.

'God, yes!' His arms tightened about her. 'Wouldn't that be wonderful? I——'

'Zack,' Maxine appeared in the doorway of the register office, 'they're ready for us now,' she prompted.

'Damn,' he frowned. 'I haven't finished saying all that needs to be said.' He looked down at Holly.

'Tell me after the wedding,' she smiled.

He nodded reluctantly, and the two of them followed Maxine and James into the registrar's room. Despite what she had heard to the contrary about register office weddings Holly found her marriage to Zack very beautiful, deciding that it didn't really matter where the ceremony took place, as long as you married the person you loved. When Zack placed the plain gold wedding ring on her finger the tears fell softly down her cheeks, and she received his kiss as if in a dream.

But Zack still seemed tense and ill at ease as they thanked the registrar and received Maxine and James's congratulations, keeping her firmly at his side as they all turned to leave, the four of them going out to a celebration lunch before Holly and Zack went on their honeymoon.

Holly came to an abrupt halt as she saw the woman sitting at the back of the room where she had just been married, all colour leaving her face. She was a little older now, the red hair showing signs of greying, but despite the five years since she had last seen her Holly knew that this was her mother! What was she doing here on *her* wedding day?

CHAPTER TEN

'MAXINE and I will wait for you at our flat,' James told Zack softly before leaving.

Holly turned from staring at her mother to look at Zack. 'I—You knew she was going to be here?'

He nodded. 'I invited her.'

'Why?' she choked.

'Holly——'

'This is our wedding day, Zack,' she cried. 'You promised me you would only ever try to make me happy.'

'I will——'

'By inviting my mother here?' There were tears in her eyes. 'How could you do this to me, Zack?'

'Darling——'

'Holly,' a quietly firm voice broke into their heated conversation, her mother having approached them without either of them being aware of it. 'Zack invited me to your wedding because I asked him to.'

Holly turned to look at her mother, seeing the pain etched beside the violet eyes, the once beautiful face shadowed in sadness. And Holly knew she had been the one to put the pain and sadness there.

'Let's get out of here and go somewhere more private,' rasped Zack, the only one conscious that they weren't alone.

'I'd rather not,' Holly said stiffly.

His mouth firmed tautly. 'You just promised to obey me, Holly,' he reminded her abruptly. 'Are you breaking that vow already?'

She was very pale, still suffering from the shock of her mother being here. 'You know I'm not,' she had chosen to keep obey in their wedding ceremony. 'But——'

'Then trust me,' he prompted softly. 'Just trust me in this.'

She gave another reluctant glance at her mother, seeing only gentle understanding in her face. 'I trust you with my life, Zack, you know that——'

'Then trust me with your happiness too,' he said grimly.

She allowed herself to be led from the building and out to James's car that he had left for them in the car park, almost numb as Zack helped her mother into the back seat before opening Holly's door. She was so tense on the drive to their apartment that she felt almost as if she might break in two, her thoughts all running into each other, and none of them making sense.

Zack ignored the champagne they had left waiting for them, pouring three glasses of brandy instead, and drinking his own down in one swallow. Holly ignored her own glass, although she noticed her mother took several reviving sips of hers. She didn't know what her mother had to feel nervous about. Unless Zack had forced her to come here, although they had both denied that.

'Right,' Zack said briskly. 'I'm going to tell you why I invited your mother to our wedding, Holly, and then I'm going to leave the two of you alone to talk.'

'No——'

'Please, Holly,' her mother softly interrupted her forceful refusal. 'We do need to talk.'

'What about?' she snapped.

Her mother flinched. 'So many things, so many misunderstandings.'

Holly turned away. 'I can't imagine what, I'm sure we've always understood each other perfectly!'

'Holly,' Zack reprimanded gently. 'Your mother didn't reject you five years ago.'

'Then she gave a very good impression of it!'

He sighed. 'Will you just stop being on the defensive and listen for a few minutes——'

'It's all right, Zack,' surprisingly it was her mother who once again cut into the conversation. 'Could you just leave us alone together for a while?'

He looked undecided for a few moments, and then he nodded, coming over to kiss Holly on her stiff lips. 'I'd never hurt you, Holly,' he told her huskily. 'And I would never let anyone else hurt you either. Please, just listen to your mother, give her a chance to explain.'

Holly stared coldly at her mother once they were alone. The older woman possessed a fragile beauty that hadn't been there five years ago, as if she had suffered greatly during those years. 'If you've come to ruin my marriage as I once ruined yours then I think I should tell you you've succeeded. I'll never forgive Zack for this,' she said dully.

'Oh, Holly!' her mother's face crumpled emotionally. 'Did we do this to you?'

'Not "we", Mother, just you.'

'But I never realised, Holly, don't you know that?'

Her mouth twisted derisively. 'You rejected me from your life and now claim you didn't know how hurt and bewildered I'd been? Really, Mother, that's expecting too much!'

'I didn't reject you,' her mother told her heatedly. 'I never rejected you!'

'How long is it since I last saw you, Mother?' Holly asked pointedly.

The violet eyes so like her own flashed with a temper

similar to hers too. 'And whose decision has that been?' she demanded to know.

Holly's eyes widened. 'You surely aren't blaming me for that?' she gasped.

'Who else? I wrote to you, Holly, time and time again, until in the end you used to send the letters back to me unopened.'

Holly turned away. 'We had nothing to say to each other then, and we haven't now either.'

'Holly——'

'I don't know why Zack got in touch with you,' she said flatly. 'But I know exactly why you came today, although I never thought of you as vindictive. This should have been the most beautiful day of my entire life, instead it's turned out to be a nightmare.'

'Zack came to see me because he was concerned for you, because he loves you.'

'He has a strange way of showing it!' Pain twisting her heart until it was all she could feel.

'Holly,' her mother's voice was edged with her own pain, 'have you always been this bitter?'

'Only since my mother believed it when she was told I was a whore!' rasped Holly.

All colour seemed to fade from her mother's face, leaving her ghostly pale. 'I never believed that of you,' she said quietly. 'Alex raped you, I knew that.'

Holly's eyes widened disbelievingly. 'You *knew?*' she gasped.

Her mother nodded. 'I should have seen it coming, I suppose,' she spoke softly, almost to herself. 'You were together such a lot, and Alex had always been wild——'

'Wild?' Holly blinked her puzzlement at the description. 'He never seemed that way to me.'

'Giles had a lot of trouble with him after his mother died, although he seemed to settle down a little once he went to college. I mistakenly thought his innocent friendship with you was a good sign,' she sighed.

'But the night—that night,' Holly bit out tautly. 'You never said a word, you just believed what Alex said about me.'

Her mother shook her head. 'I didn't speak because I knew the truth and I thought you'd been through enough for one night. After you'd gone to bed that night I told Giles that either Alex went out of our lives or I divorced him. I never knew that you thought I believed you guilty all this time,' she said in an anguished voice. 'I thought you blamed me for letting it happen, I thought *that* was why you returned my letters, why you disappeared so completely once you left school.'

'Why should I blame you?' Holly asked dazedly. 'What could you have done about it?'

'I don't know, but I've always felt responsible. Until Zack came to see me I truly believed you wanted nothing to do with me because you blamed me for what Alex did to you.'

Holly felt stunned, hardly able to believe her mother was telling the truth even now. 'You could have visited me at the school, Mother,' she returned flatly. 'Could have made me listen.'

'Miss Oakridge advised me not to force you to see me, she said you still weren't ready for that, and that if I did visit you I could make things worse.'

'Miss Oakridge knew about—about Alex?' Her former headmistress had never given any indication that she did.

'Yes,' her mother confirmed. 'When the doctor told me he thought it best if you went back to school, away from where it had happened, I had to tell your headmistress so that she could keep an eye on you. If you knew how much it hurt me to send you away like that!' Tears glistened in her eyes. 'I needed you then as much as you say you needed me, but in the circumstances, Alex being your stepbrother, the doctor felt it best that you went away. As I went ahead with the divorce proceedings I knew he'd been right. Giles was angry, I was bitter, the whole thing turned into an ugly fight.'

'And yet you still stayed close to Bobbie—Roberta.' That was another pain Holly had never got over, her mother choosing the other girl over her own daughter.

'Bobbie had no idea what had happened between you and Alex,' her mother reasoned. 'And I'd been the only mother she'd known for two years. Both Giles and I agreed that she should remain innocent of the facts, that she should stay out of our battle.'

'Is that why you were coming to collect her from school and not me?'

'I was coming for you both, as you would have known if you hadn't kept returning my letters. In the end I gave up writing, hoping to put things right between us when you came home. Do you know how hurt I was that you chose to go to friends or stay at school during the holidays?'

Holly was confused, not knowing what to believe any more. For five years she had thought her mother blamed her for the break-up of her marriage, had blamed herself for it, and all the time she had been wrong about how her mother felt. 'Mother, I—— How do you feel about me now?'

'The same as I always have,' her mother answered quietly. 'I love you. You're my daughter.'

Holly moistened her dry lips. 'And does Zack—does he know all this already?'

'Yes. You don't seriously think he would let me

anywhere near you if he thought I would hurt you in any way?' her mother chided. 'Zack loves you, Holly, he only wants your happiness. I believe he thought that I was a shadow in your life that would always be painful for you. But I can see he was wrong. Whatever misunderstandings we had in the past it's too late to undo them now.' She turned to leave.

'No!' Holly cried desperately. 'No, don't go,' she asked as her mother turned back to her. 'Zack was right,' she said haltingly. 'I've let what happened shape my life. I—I'd like to get to know you again, Mother.' She looked at her with pleading eyes.

Suddenly they were in each other's arms, crying and laughing at the same time, both talking at once.

'Holly . . .?' Zack burst in from the kitchen, his eyes opening wide as he saw the two women hugging each other, relief flooding through him as he saw the elation in Holly's face. 'I thought the two of you had come to blows,' he admitted ruefully.

'Come and join us, darling.' Holly held her arms out to him. 'I want to introduce you to my mother.' As she watched the pride in his eyes as he approached them she knew that in that moment his love for her had grown. Maybe because *she* had finally grown, at last.

'Did I remember to thank you?'

Zack looked up at her sleepily as the two of them lay in bed together later that night. Their honeymoon was being spent in romantic Paris, in a house Zack had loaned from a friend. 'For what?' he asked indulgently.

'For giving me back my mother.' The three of them had finally joined Maxine and James for lunch, and she had later parted from her mother with a promise to see her as soon as they returned from their honeymoon.

'Are you going to give all my life that "happy-ever-after" touch?' she teased.

'I'm going to try,' he promised.

'How did you know, Zack?' She lay against his chest during this needed respite from their tempestuous lovemaking. 'What made you realise I'd been wrong about my mother?'

'I didn't.' He idly played with the hair at her nape. 'I just wondered if she might be interested in the fact that we were getting married. She was. She went on to tell me her side of things, and I thought the two of you should meet. I tried to tell you before the wedding, but then I thought perhaps you wouldn't marry me. I daren't risk that, not after losing you once already.'

'I love you more than ever for giving me back my mother.'

'Only for that?'

Her hands roamed caressingly down his body. 'Well, maybe for one or two other reasons too.'

'I should think so,' he growled.

'Isn't it time you "worshipped me with your body" again?' She looked at him with innocent eyes.

Zack smiled. 'I thought you were never going to ask!'

Coming Next Month in Harlequin Presents!

775 RAGE TO POSSESS Jayne Bauling
It's hard to be objective in affairs of the heart. But that's no excuse
for a war correspondent to blame an *Afrinews* photographer for
the strain on his best friend's marriage.

776 NUMBER ONE Donna Huxley
No one offers an injured American golfer any chance of ever
walking again, let alone winning her next LPGA tournament—
except one incredibly dynamic man who knows the psychology of
winning. But does it work with love?

777 THE FRENCHMAN'S KISS Claudia Jameson
After he labels her brother as unworthy of his sister's hand, how
can a wealthy French auto designer expect a young travel agent to
believe his intentions toward her would be honorable?

778 OUT OF THIS DARKNESS Madeleine Ker
The score is far from settled, when a dashing London lawyer
outsmarts a sexy magazine editor and save his client's reputation,
only to become the central figure in a case of love versus desire.

779 LOVE'S TANGLED WEB Mary Lyons
Why a wealthy Sicilian count would offer a fortune for their
rundown Suffolk estate and allow himself to be tricked into
marriage, she does not know. Then somehow he arranges to marry
her, instead of her sister.

780 A PAST REVENGE Carole Mortimer
An up-and-coming artist has every reason to resist the lethal
charm of an arrogant oil tycoon, who commissions her to paint his
mistress's portrait. Unlike him, she can't forget his treatment of
her seven years ago . . . .

781 HAD WE NEVER LOVED Jeneth Murrey
She left his Highland castle right after their wedding five years ago,
and her feelings haven't changed. She won't go back to him—not
until his love for her outweighs his belief in her guilt.

782 THE DEVIL'S PAWN Yvonne Whittal
Unless a South African construction magnate makes room in his
heart for love, his wife will never feel she's anything more to him
than the daughter of the man he despises—a pawn in a deadly
game of revenge!

What romance fans
say about Harlequin…

"Harlequins are the best."
—D.L.,* Tampa, Florida

"Excellent…very good reading."
—K.R.P., Burlington, Vermont

"…fresh and original…tremendously
romantic."
—F.V., Abbotsford, British Columbia

"…Harlequin makes me relax and
dream a little."
—S.L., Aurora, North Carolina

*Names available on request.

Take these
4 best-selling novels
FREE

Your FREE gift includes

Anne Mather—Born out of Love
Violet Winspear—Time of the Temptress
Charlotte Lamb—Man's World
Sally Wentworth—Say Hello to Yesterday